MW01539678

Happy reading!

Kristi Hole

2003

Happy reading!

Best, [signature]

2003

Stage
Fright

Kristi D. Holl

Mid-Prairie Books
Parkersburg, Iowa

Books in the Carousel Mystery Series:

A Spin Out of Control

Deadly Disguise

Stage Fright

Printed in the United States of America.

Published by: Mid-Prairie Books
                P.O. Box 680
                Parkersburg IA 50665

ISBN 0-931209-89-7

98 99 00 01 02   5 4 3 2 1

For Cheryl,
a dear friend and "sister"

I would like to thank Mary Navratil and Todd Thorson for their help in producing this book:

To **Mary Navratil**, the director of *Annie, jr.*, for her extensive information about producing children's theatre in general, and *Annie, jr.* in particular.

To **Todd Thorson**, owner of the Story Theatre-Grand Opera House, for allowing me to explore the fascinating nooks and crannies of the theatre in order to accurately portray it in the book.

Their help was much appreciated!

Table of Contents

CHAPTER ONE

"Center of Attention"

Lauren Burk shivered when she stepped into the dark inner lobby of the Story Theatre-Grand Opera House. "I wish someone would turn the lights on. I can almost believe those creepy phantom stories are true!" she whispered.

Carl stepped on Lauren's heel, pulling off her shoe, and growled deep in his throat. "I am . . . the Phantom of the Opera *House*," he hissed, pulling his winter coat up over his head like a cape.

Lauren groaned. "That's terrible, Carl. Come on."

Together they crossed the shadowy inner lobby, following the echoes of children's voices into the main theatre. More than thirty kids crowded around the play director down near the front of the stage. It was the Friday before Thanksgiving, and the junior theatre troupe was being given a tour of the opera house, where their play would be performed the following weekend.

"Save your voices, kids," Mrs. D. called, standing in a small pool of light. "We won't rehearse today, but I want to show you the layout of the stage and dressing rooms."

"Mrs. D!" Leesa Lyons piped up. "I invented a great song and dance routine to perform just before the play starts. I brought my tap shoes with me." She held them high and waved them. "Should I get up on stage now and show you?"

Carl nearly choked on his gum. "You're not doing any solo, Twinkle Toes. What a way to clear the theatre. Small childen will run screaming into the frozen night air, frantic parents—"

"Oh, shut up." Leesa swung her taps shoes and smacked him squarely in the back. "I wasn't talking to you." Her lower jaw jutted forward aggressively.

Lauren smothered a smile, then glanced across the jostling group of kids. A curly-haired six-foot-tall ninth grader named Nick winked at her and rolled his eyes. His mouth was wide and straight, turning lopsided when he smiled. Lauren grinned back, aware of a fluttering under her ribcage.

"Who's that?" Carl asked.

"Who?"

"That guy you're making eyes at."

Lauren elbowed Carl in the side. "That's Nick. He lives on my block. Moved in with his aunt and uncle a while back." Lauren shifted her backpack to a more comfortable position. "His collie got loose and ended up on our porch one night. I met him when he came looking for him."

"I never noticed him at rehearsals before."

"He's not an actor. He's Assistant Stage Manager." Lauren tried to sound casual, but her voice squeaked. "He'll be moving heavy props and stuff like that." She smiled again at Nick. "He's in high school and wrestles."

"A real Mr. Perfect." Carl leaned close.

"Lauren's got a crush on Saint Nick," he whispered. "Hey! Saint Nick, get it?"

Mrs. D. snapped her fingers. "Listen, kids. Let's do the tour, then we'll discuss your idea, Leesa." She jumped up lightly and perched on the edge of the stage, the brilliant red scalloped curtain a perfect backdrop for her quilted black jacket and black hair. "First, you all need to understand what a privilege it is to perform *Annie, jr.* on this stage. The Story Theatre-Opera House is on the National Register of Historic Places and has been operating since 1913. As an opera house, it was built to hold 400 chairs with hat racks underneath. Some of these original seats are still here in the theatre."

"What about the phantom?" Carl called out.

"Carl, please." Mrs. D. shook her head. "Behind me on the stage, behind the curtain, is the theatre screen where you watch movies every week. Right now, though, the screen and speakers are raised high to expose the stage where we'll perform. The theatre opened in December, 1913, with the melodrama stage play *The Two Orphans.*"

"That's why we're doing a play about Little Orphan Annie?"

"No, it's just a coincidence," Mrs. D. said. "At first movies alternated with live stage productions, until the live acting became too expensive. At one point, the stage was closed for 40 years! It was restored in the '80's, and the original orchestra pit was uncovered and rebuilt in 1990."

"My mom was in *The Sound of Music* here," little Julia piped up. An Alice-in-Wonderland type, Julia had big eyes and long straight hair. "I got to sit in the front row."

"Yes, the adults perform every June during Scandinavian Days, and our children's theatre production is for the Christmas Yulefest celebration." Mrs. D. hopped down lightly from the edge of the stage. "And now, for a short tour."

"But I'm scared of the phantom!" Carl's eyes rolled back in his head, revealing white eyeballs. "What if he's hiding backstage?"

Lauren glanced up and caught Nick peering at her. A smile flickered at his lips. Flustered, Lauren pretended to be fascinated by Mrs. D.'s little speech.

Mrs. D. sighed. "All right, I'll tell you where the phantom rumors started, but then I don't want to hear another thing about it."

"Cross my heart and hope to die." Carl made a big X in the area of his heart, right across his T-shirt's bold red letters: *I intend to live forever! (So far, so good.)*

"One morning over a year ago, Mr. Thorson, who now owns the theatre, was backstage. As he climbed to one of the dressing rooms above, he glanced to the stage below and spotted a glove lying there. Mr. Thorson did not believe in phantoms, however," she said sternly, looking pointedly at Carl.

Jill Cline raised her hand. "Whose glove was it?" asked the star of the play.

"Mr. Thorson knew it belonged to Dick Peterson, the former owner who still lived upstairs in the apartment above the theatre. Mr. Thorson knew that Mr. Peterson would never leave the glove there—he was too careful to keep things neat and spotless. So Todd—Mr. Thorson, that is—glanced down in front of the stage. Mr. Peterson lay over here—" she pointed "—on the floor, where he'd fallen the night before."

"Maybe the phantom pushed him!" Carl suggested.

"You're cruisin' for a bruisin', Carl," Mrs. D. warned. "No, the phantom didn't push him. I understand that he tripped over the footlights." She pointed to the row of colored lights at the edge of the stage. "The fall was serious. Soon after that Mr. Peterson moved to Bethany Manor. He is truly the expert on our theatre. He put together twenty-three notebooks full of artifacts, movie posters, and photos of the theatre."

"But what about the weird things people have seen in the theatre? That doesn't explain—"

"Not another word, Carl." She shook her head firmly, her shoulder-length hair swinging side to side. "They're just silly stories."

"Mrs. Deeeeeeeeee!" Leesa interrupted in a voice so nasal it sounded as if she had a clothespin on her nose. "Can I show you my song and tap routine now? It'd be the perfect kick-off for the show."

Lauren tried not to roll her eyes. From things said at school, she knew Leesa was still fuming that she wasn't playing Annie, and was only one of the large Orphan Chorus like most of them. Trust her to try to steal the limelight before the play even started.

"Let's do the tour first, Leesa," Mrs. D. said, glancing at her watch. "Oops! We must move quickly. I need to leave by four." She motioned them to follow her to the door at the side of the stage. "We go through here and up some steps."

Lauren poked Carl in the arm. "I need to get out

of here soon too." She shifted her backpack to a more comfortable spot, remembering the cash stuffed down in the bottom. "I'm going to the bank after this to put more catering money in savings."

"Do you have enough for that present yet?"

"Almost." Lauren grinned. "I can't *wait* to see Mom's face on Christmas morning!"

Lauren and Carl both worked on weekends for Lauren's parents, the owners of the new Carousel Catering Service. Lauren's mom did the cooking and baking, but Lauren and Carl helped with simple preparations, then acted as waiters and servers at various events. Her mom worked night and day, sometimes seven days a week, and Lauren had figured out the perfect Christmas present for her.

As soon as she had another five dollars, she could pay for the Blue Willow serving platter she'd found in the antique store uptown. It would replace the smashed one that had belonged to her mom's grandmother. Every year the old blue and white platter, with the tiny Chinese figures on it, had held Thanksgiving turkeys, Christmas hams, and Fourth of July pinwheel cookies.

Last year at Christmas, Lauren's older brother Shawn had thrown a fit just as her mom carried in the ham. Her mom had dropped the ham, smashing the platter against the kitchen's tile countertop. Her mom hadn't been able to glue it together, and had cried as she'd cleaned up the pieces. In October Lauren had spotted a Blue Willow platter just like it in the antique store and started saving money to buy it.

"The kitchen calendar is full of Christmas parties in December, so I should have the rest of the money in a few days."

"Hi, Lauren." Lauren jumped as Nick spoke directly over her shoulder. "I didn't know you were in the play." He took a step closer to her and bent forward, lowering his voice. "You should be Annie."

Lauren felt a blush crawling up her neck. "I'm just one of the singing orphans." She glanced up at Nick's laughing eyes and big grin, then felt her blush spread up her face. He sure was *tall*, Lauren thought, and so muscular compared to the boys her age.

Nick laid his hands on her shoulders. "Everybody's important, Lauren, even the chorus. That's what my aunt says. According to her, being Assistant Stage Manager means I practically run the show."

I wouldn't mind if you ran the show, Lauren thought, her knees a little weak. Aloud, she said, "Nick, this is my friend, Carl Harris. He's in seventh grade too."

Carl saluted smartly, then bowed. "Carl's my name, entertainment's my game."

"And he has the detention to prove it!" Lauren grinned. "He spends classtime entertaining everybody."

"Now, now," Carl said, hanging his head in mock embarrassment. "You're too kind."

Nick brushed his hand over his curly hair. "Well, I'm not too entertaining, but I like *being* entertained. I love this old theatre. I helped my friend Jake in the concession room once, and then Todd let me watch the new Star Wars movie for free."

"Come *on*, you guys," Leesa called, skipping over

to take Nick's arm. "You'll miss the tour." She dimpled up at the tall high schooler. "Hi. We haven't met. I know because I'd remember you." She blinked and dimpled again. "I'm Leesa Lyons, and we'll be working together closely. Can you make sure the spotlights are focused on me during my whole introduction? I'll be dancing all over the stage and need someone to keep up with me." She stroked his arm, which she held in a vise-like grip. "*Oooohh!* I'm sure we'll get along just fine."

Nick backed away, slowly removing his arm from her grasp. "I'd be glad to help you, but I don't do the lights. I work with the backdrops and flats, raising and lowering scenery."

"Flats?"

"Those wooden frames with material stretched across them. You know, with those scenes painted on them."

"Oh." Leesa's lower lip shot out, then she grabbed his arm again. "I'm sure we'll be great friends anyway."

Lauren gritted her teeth. Did Leesa have to be center stage *all* the time? Bristling, she followed Nick and Leesa backstage, with Carl whistling "We Wish You a Merry Christmas" off-key right behind her.

"Stay with me and watch your feet." Backstage, Mrs. D. skirted around two beat-up metal trash cans, props for *Annie, jr.* "You can look around, but please don't touch things. The valuable posters and props—like that Cathedral radio and old hat tree— are 'hands off'."

Near the back wall, Lauren studied the yellowed hand-printed signs: "No Swearing!" and "No-

Spiting-on-the-Floor!" She grinned. Somebody back then couldn't spell. Underneath was an orange "No Smoking!" sign next to a red fire extinguisher. She could sure understand that: everything in the theatre was wood and cloth. On Lauren's right were plastic-encased posters, one advertising "Our first movie! *Birth of A Nation*." The next poster was for *Cleopatra* with Claudette Colbert, a woman wearing a ton of eye makeup.

"Who's that?" Carl asked. "She's got two black eyes."

Lauren shrugged. She'd never heard of that actress, nor the homely actor on the next poster: Humphrey Bogart in *Maltese Falcon*. She shook her head. Homely Humphrey would never make it in today's movies.

Lauren turned and bumped into Leesa, who stood right behind her. "Hey, watch it!" Leesa snarled, studying herself in an old full-length mirror nailed to the wall. Just above Leesa was a handprinted 1946 sign announcing that *The Bells of St. Mary's* would be playing there for five days in April.

Mrs. D. reached behind her, pressed a button, and the red scalloped curtain slowly rose, revealing rows of empty seats below the stage. When the curtain was up, she stepped from the wings onto the stage and pointed to the back of the theatre. "The light booth and sound booth are up there in the center of the balcony. The sound booth is on the left, by the fire escape. Our sound and lights managers will join us for rehearsal tomorrow afternoon."

Lauren gazed around backstage in awe. It must be two stories high, she thought, craning her neck to study the odd things hanging overhead. The movie screen and speakers were suspended near the front of the stage. Behind it were row upon row of painted movie backdrops hanging near the ceiling. One showed brick stores with flower boxes, one backdrop looked like a library with doors and painted-on bookshelves. One huge suspended sign said ASCOT.

"Carl, look!" She pointed to a small artificial Christmas tree hanging upside down high overhead. Its red balls and silver tinsel shimmered. "Mrs. D., what's a tree doing there?"

Mrs. D. grinned. "In *My Fair Lady* we used that tree, with its tinsel and white lights, as a chandelier. It was lowered down during the ballroom scene." She did a quick waltz around the stage. "It's up there in case we ever need another chandelier. The ASCOT sign was from the scene at the horse races."

"Isn't this cool?" Jill asked Lauren. She pointed at stairs on each side of the stage that led to doors above. "Where do those go?" she asked the director.

Mrs. D. moved the antique wheelchair aside and pointed to her left. "That one leads to the Greta Garbo dressing room." She paused, then sighed when at least five people asked, *Who?* "Greta Garbo was a famous actress, a very mysterious woman, and there are six posters of her in that tiny dressing room." She swung around and pointed to the stairs on her right. "Those lead to another dressing room. There you'll find posters of Elvis, the King of rock and roll, plus one of King Kong."

Carl saluted. "Long live the kings!"

Mrs. D. flipped a switch that suddenly lit up the

stage. "Over on the far wall is the theatre's old light board, with switches that pull up and down. That's how the lights used to be turned on and off, but it's disconnected now."

"Hey!" Leesa's shout echoed from above.

About twenty heads swiveled around in unison. At the top of the stairs to the Garbo dressing room, Leesa stood with hands on hips. "This is a *dinky* room. I'll need one this size all for myself. And the lighting! I can't possibly put on makeup in here."

Mrs. D. cleared her throat loud enough for Lauren to hear clear across the stage. "Please come down, Leesa. The dressing rooms are reserved for the stars of the play. The Orphan Chorus and gymnasts will do makeup in another large room. Let me show you how to get there."

She parted the group of kids to walk down several steps to a door marked EXIT. "This door goes outside at the back of the theatre." She pushed it open and held it. "Next door you can see the back of City Hall. We use their large basement during performances for a dressing area and makeup room. If you need special makeup, like false hair or a beard, a Makeup Mom will assist you. Most of you will get made up and wait there until someone collects you when it's time to perform."

Leesa's voice was so whiny that it make Lauren wince. "But Mrs. D., it's *cold* out there. The forecast said *snow* next week."

"Afraid you'll freeze your dainty tootsies?" Carl asked.

"Oh, shut up," Leesa snapped, swinging around so hard that her heart pendant hit her cheek.

"Kids, kids." Mrs. D. shut the door. "It's barely

twenty feet from door to door, only a five-second
dash even in a blizzard." She motioned for everyone
to come down the short flight of steps to the main
theatre, where she began handing out the final
week's rehearsal schedule. "That's all for tonight,"
she said two minutes later. "Remember, our first
rehearsal onstage is tomorrow afternoon at two.
Please be prompt and—"

"Wait!" a voice yelled. "It's showtime!"

Lauren whirled around. From behind the beige
curtain on the other side of the stage, a black patent
leather shoe appeared first, followed by a thin leg in
a white stocking. Next came a red leotard topped by
a stiff red tutu and sparkly vest. Leesa cartwheeled
to center stage, her hair covered by a multi-colored
clown wig. In her arms she clutched a ragged
stuffed dog.

Lauren covered her mouth, but the giggles
escaped through her fingers. Oh, this was really too
much.

"Now, you'll have to use your imagination this
time, everybody. This is Little Orphan Annie's dog,
Sandy. At the performance, I'll wear Annie's red
dress instead of my old dance outfit, plus Annie's
red wig, but at least you can get the idea." Clip-clipping across the stage, Leesa yanked a tape player
out of her book bag and set it down near the edge of
the stage.

"I've called this 'Sandy's Song,'" she said, then
pressed a button. The theatre was instantly filled
with tinny, off-key marching band music. Hands on
hips and tutu bouncing, Leesa strutted up and
down the stage, flinging the poor stuffed dog around
like a baton.

Most of the audience hooting was drowned out by the music. Looking stunned, Mrs. D. sank down in a front row seat. Lauren followed Carl down off the stage to sit in the second row. She shrugged out of her backpack. "Can you believe this?" she asked, dropping her bag in the seat next to her.

After marching back and forth to the blaring music, Leesa cartwheeled to the front of the stage and held out the stuffed dog. One plastic eye was missing. With wisps of blonde hair escaping from the clown wig, Leesa opened her mouth and began to sing:

"This is my beloved Sandy,
Don't you think he's quite a dandy?"
Tap, tap-tap, tap, tap.
"Chocolate is his favorite candy,
So is mine! Now, ain't that handy?"
Tap, tap-tap, tap, tap.

"Oh, gag me," Carl whispered.
Lauren had to agree.

"Sandy dear is quite a dog,
You should see him jump a log!"
Tap, tap-tap, tap, tap.
"Along with me he loves to jog—
Then gobbles food like any hog!"
Tap, tap-tap, tap, tap.

After the second stanza, Lauren couldn't stand anymore. She leaned over Mrs. D.'s shoulder to whisper, "I'm going to the rest room. I'll be right back."

Scooting to the end of the row, she hurried up the aisle. Leesa was making a fool of herself, and even if Lauren didn't like her much, she was embarrassed for her.   Talk about being desperate for attention. Out in the lobby, Lauren opened the red door and headed down the flight of carpeted steps to the rest room in the basement.

Even though it smelled musty year-round, Lauren loved that rest room. Everything in the little sitting room was antique and painted red and white. The wicker couch along one wall was red, with half-circle white tables at each end. A red and white rocker sat under an oval mirror, beside a white spindle table.

Lauren bent over the water fountain next to the sink and watched the water jet up, then splash back into the round porcelain bowl.

She studied her face in the oval mirror, trying to decide if the gap between her front teeth was closing or not.   Then after another quick sip, she trudged back up the stairs to the lobby.   Surely Leesa was done wailing by now. At the top of the stairs, she turned out the light, then started down the long aisle toward the now empty stage.

Without warning, the floodlights went out, plunging the stage area into darkness. A blood-curdling scream ripped through the blackened theatre.

CHAPTER TWO

"Surprise!"

Another shriek was followed by whimpering of the youngest cast members. "What's going on?" Leesa's voice screeched. "Turn the lights back on!"

"Quiet, everyone! Stay where you are," called Mrs. D. "I'll have the lights back on in just a few seconds. Please stay calm. You older kids help the little ones."

Lauren backed into a theater seat and banged her leg, then turned and groped for the doorway. When her fingers touched it, she leaned against it gratefully. She thought briefly of crawling across the lobby toward the exit—and sunlight—but decided to play it safe. Lauren hunched her shoulders and hugged herself tightly. Much as she loved the old theatre, it sure was *dark* in there. She had the uncanny feeling that she was being sucked into the blackness of the room.

The whimpering stopped, and quiet descended. Lauren frowned and gazed upward, peering through the blackness. Were those footsteps she heard overhead?

Closing her eyes to concentrate, she listened as

the footsteps grew fainter and then disappeared. Who was up there in the dark balcony? Mrs. D. had said the sound and light managers weren't coming till Saturday. Wasn't that apartment over the theatre empty?

Someone—or something—had sure been in the light room just now. From the sounds of the retreating footsteps, whoever it was could have slipped down the west side balcony stairs. Or, Lauren wondered with a shiver, did phantoms simply float wherever they had to go?

Just then someone brushed against her. Lauren gasped, then stifled a scream.

"Oh, dear, who is it?" came Mrs. D.'s voice.

"Me. Lauren. I just came up from the rest room."

"You gave me quite a fright. Wait here while I grope my way upstairs and turn these lights back on, if I can. I suppose we blew a fuse or something. You okay?"

"Sure. I'm fine." Lauren wondered if she should mention the soft footsteps she'd heard overhead, then decided against it. The way it echoed in this cavernous theatre, that noise could have come from anywhere.

She heard Mrs. D. remove the thick velvet rope that closed off the balcony stairs, then kick the small "Balcony Closed" sign that always rested on the step. Eyes closed, Lauren followed the director's movements as she slowly climbed the winding carpeted steps, then opened the door to the light booth above. Fifteen seconds later the stage lights and house lights both came up. It was like watching the sun rise in time-lapse photography.

A collective sigh floated up from the group huddled near the stage.

"What happened?"   "Is it the phantom?" "Probably the ghost of some dead actor floating around."

Leesa strutted around, *clip-clipping* her tap shoes up on stage. "Well, whoever it was, it wasn't funny. Now I'll have to start my routine over—"

A roar of protests drowned her out. Leesa ripped off her clown wig and scowled at them all. Then she spotted Nick and crooked her finger at him. Lauren chewed her lower lip and watched. Rubbing the back of his neck, Nick shuffled over to the edge of the stage. "What?" he asked suspiciously.

"Help me down." Leesa grabbed her tape player and squatted, ready to jump into Nick's arms. Lauren held her breath, hoping Nick missed catching her and Leesa splatted flat on the floor.

"Wait," Nick said. "You'd better use the stairs. You could get hurt."

"Nicky!"   Leesa's dimples worked overtime. "You're a big strong wrestler. I *know* you can catch me."

"Well . . ." Nick reached up and gripped her hands to steady her when she jumped. He let go as soon as she landed, but Leesa grabbed his arm as if she were about to topple over.

"Oh, brother," Lauren muttered miserably as she lifted her backpack, "let me out of here."

Carl grabbed his coat and followed. "Get me away from Leapin' Leesa."

They pushed through the few kids still waiting to talk to the director about their parts, strode up the aisle, through the inner lobby and outer lobby, then out into the weak November sunshine. Half a block away, Lauren glanced up at the clock on the bank: **3:52**.

"Good, there's still time," she said.

Inside the bank, Lauren found a savings deposit slip at the counter. Using a ballpoint pen attached by a chain, she carefully filled out her name and address and account number. "Santa Claus is coming to town," she sang under her breath.

"So when can you go buy that platter?" Carl asked.

"Counting this money, I only need five more dollars," Lauren said. "My mom's going to be totally blown away. The one she broke was in her family for about a hundred years, and I know she never expected to have another one."

Sliding her backpack off her shoulder, she set it on the green tiled floor and unfastened the strap. Digging under her social studies and math books, she found her wallet where she'd buried it under her gym clothes that morning. You couldn't be too careful, Lauren thought. She marched up to the window with her wallet and deposit slip.

"Hello, Lauren," the young woman at the window said. "Haven't seen you for a while. Are you taking out or putting in today?"

"Putting fifty in." Lauren handed her deposit slip to the teller and opened her wallet. She stared, blinked once, blinked again, then dropped to the floor with her backpack.

"What's with you?" Carl asked.

"Nothing. My money fell out in my bag." Lauren pulled out her books and wrinkled gym clothes, a flattened Hot Tamale box, her strawberry lip gloss, her dad's calculator and a leaky pen. Finally she turned the backpack over and shook it. Lint and two paper clips fell out, but no money. "I don't understand," she said, rocking back on her heels.

"Are you sure the money was in there today?" Carl asked.

"I know it was." Lauren chewed her lower lip, biting hard to keep from crying. "I kept my bag with me all day too. I only set it down at lunch long enough to get my food. I wasn't gone five minutes."

"Not too smart, sorry to say." Carl checked her two zippered outside pockets. "Did you wear it in class all day? Maybe somebody sitting behind you lifted it out."

"I would have felt somebody doing that." Lauren hugged her knees, and her blonde hair fell over her face. "It must have been at lunch." She looked up then, pounding her fist on her knee. "First, my gym shoes stolen last month. Now *this*. I worked *hard* for that money."

The teller leaned out over the counter, tapping her lavender lips with a long fingernail of the exact same color. "Can I help?" she asked. "We're about to close."

Lauren sighed. "No, I'll have to come back when I find my money." Stuffing her books and clothes back in her bag, Lauren dragged it by the shoulder strap as she trudged out of the bank.

Lauren had plodded halfway home before she remembered her bike was still at the high school. She attended middle school in the nearby small town of Roland, the other town in their school district, but she biked to the Story City high school to catch the bus every day. Today the *Annie, jr.* cast had all walked uptown together after getting off the bus, and she'd left her bike behind.

"We forgot our bikes," she said. "How could a day that started off so good get so crummy?"

"Never fear, Carl's here." He bowed from the waist, and his purple ear muffs fell off. "I'll sing to you and cheer you up. Let's see. *'You'd better not shout, you'd better not cry, you'd better not pout, I'm telling you why . . .'*" Carl warbled, holding a red pencil for a microphone as he sang into the eraser.

"Carl, stop," Lauren begged. "People are watching us."

"I bet you'd rather hear about Jolly Old St. Nick, our macho wrestler. Am I right? Ho, ho, ho!"

"Please! Not in public."

"Just trying to cheer you up. Wait. I know." He fluffed up his hair till it bushed out around his head, tied his jacket around his hips like a skirt, then tap danced down the sidewalk. "Remind you of anyone we love to hate?"

Lauren burst out laughing. Crazy or not, Carl had a way of making her problems smaller. Ten minutes later, they'd retrieved their bikes and headed their separate ways.

At home Lauren leaned her bike with its wobbly kick stand up against the house, then crunched through brown curled-up maple leaves to their porch. Her mind on the missing money, she barely noticed the withered marigolds or bronze-colored mums that still bloomed along the south side of the house.

Inside, Lauren dropped her bag by the door and headed to the cozy kitchen, her mouth watering at the warm, sugary smells. There, her mom was chopping raisins on a cutting board. "Whatcha making?" she asked, pulling up a stool and perching on it.

"*Julekake* for Mrs. Doolittle's Christmas brunch tomorrow."

"What's that?"

"Norwegian yeast bread full of raisins and currants." She scraped the chopped fruit into a bowl, then set the cutting board in the sink. "I already made the *sandbakkels* and spritz cookies. I'll make rosettes tomorrow. All traditional Norwegian goodies."

"Makes me hungry. Want me to taste test anything?"

"Sure, but just one of each." She reached into the huge catering refrigerator for a pound of butter. "I'll bake the apple-cinnamon muffins in the morning, plus cut up the fruit salad. Can you still help tomorrow?"

"Sure. Rehearsal isn't till two, Mrs. D. said." Elbow on the counter, Lauren leaned her chin on her palm. She gazed around the spotless kitchen, from the crowded calendar on the bulletin board to the sign on the wall that warned: **If in doubt, throw it out!**

"I'm glad we're catering your cast party next weekend. That'll be fun!" Lauren's mom stopped creaming butter and sugar to study her daughter's face. "Bad rehearsal tonight? You look down in the dumps."

"Wasn't really a rehearsal, just a meeting to show us around backstage. The only disgusting part was when Leesa performed a dumb song and dance show she made up. In a tutu with a stuffed dog! She can't stand that she's just a common orphan, like most of us. She invented something to perform *before* the show starts. It stunk like a *skunk.*"

Beth Burk chuckled. "I can only imagine. Still …" She paused. "You don't usually let Leesa's antics get you down anymore."

"It's not that." Lauren slouched on the stool, and her elbow slipped off the edge of the counter, jerking her chin. "When I got to the bank to deposit fifty dollars, I didn't have it anymore. It must have been stolen at school."

"Fifty dollars!" boomed a loud voice in Lauren's ear.

She jumped so far that she fell off her stool. "Shawn, don't sneak up on me like that!" Her eighteen-year-old brother yanked her hair as he swaggered into the room, dressed in short shorts and a tank top in spite of the chilly November weather. From the looks of the sweat running down his neck, he'd been lifting weights in the basement again.

"Move over, Midget." He elbowed her as he charged past. "And how's Miss Perfect, the star of the show?" he sneered, a snarl curling his lip.

"You know I'm not the star. I'm just a kid at the orphanage."

Shawn flexed his biceps, watching his Black Widow Spider tattoo ripple. "I bet everyone who tried out got a part, didn't they? Ha! They just gave you a part so your family will *pay* to see their little darling perform. I know *I'll* be there, front and center, to watch you fall flat on your face."

"Oh, Shawn, please don't come," Lauren begged.

"You won't like it. It's just a bunch of little kids singing and dancing. Mom, don't let him come."

Mrs. Burk shrugged, but didn't answer. Finally she said, "I'm really more concerned about your money that's missing."

"If I'd known you had fifty dollars, *I'd* have swiped it," Shawn said, reaching into the smaller family fridge for a can of Coke. "Then again, Shrimp, maybe I did!" He popped the tab, guzzled half the can in one gulp, then punched Lauren— hard—on the arm. "Did you guard your wallet with your life?"

"How'd you know the money was in my wallet?" Lauren demanded. "*Did* you take my money, Shawn? Is that how you paid to get your car fixed?"

Just then their father, Bill Burk, stepped out of his office in the den. "What's the trouble?" he asked, a warning clear in his voice.

"Nothing, Bill, really," Lauren's mom said, a worried pucker on her forehead. "Shawn's just teasing."

Lauren rubbed her arm where she'd been punched. "Shawn took my fifty dollars that I saved from catering."

"Shawn?" Bill Burk's voice was very low and very soft, and it made Lauren shiver. That was her dad's really *mad* voice.

"I didn't take her stupid money. Like I need it." He stomped out of the kitchen. "I get blamed for everything around here. What a dump."

Lauren slumped over at the counter, suddenly aware of a headache pounding at her temples. "I'm sorry," she said, her voice very small. "I didn't mean to cause trouble."

"You didn't, honey," her dad said. "Shawn *has* had problems with honesty in the past. Do you really think he took your money?"

Lauren sighed and rubbed her temples like she'd seen her mom do. "No, not really," she said, remembering something. "I didn't bring my bag downstairs till I left for school. I don't remember Shawn being awake when I left this morning."

"That's right," her mom interjected, relief thick in her voice. "He didn't have a class till eleven today."

Lauren's older brother was enrolled in a nearby junior college, where he commuted every day. He'd barely graduated from high school last year, and his grades stunk, so he couldn't go to the university he'd wanted. Lauren sighed again. She had counted the days till her older brother moved out. Now she didn't know when that might happen.

At least her dad worked at home now, handling the business side of the catering on his computer. With her dad in the house, Shawn didn't pull half the nasty stunts he used to. Even so, Lauren was thankful Shawn had kept his job as an orderly at Bethany Manor. He would've snarled at their catering customers and insulted people, single-handedly wrecking the business.

"Say, before I forget," Beth Burk said, "Ella stopped today and said Tillie'd like to see you sometime soon." Lauren's mom waved her wooden mixing spoon back and forth. "Something about a surprise for you."

"What kind of surprise?" Lauren asked.

"Don't know. Guess you'll have to go find out."

One last time Lauren rooted in the bottom of her

school bag, hoping against hope she'd find her
money. Papers fell from her social studies book,
including the notice handed out at school that day
about head lice. Lauren scratched the back of her
head. She hated when they got those warnings.
Her head always itched for days afterward.

Sliding from the kitchen stool, she hugged her
mom, then headed upstairs. Up in her room, she
glanced out the window and looked down on the
ranch-style house next door, where Tillie used to
live with her son, Don, and his wife, Ella. For several years, Lauren's regular Saturday morning job
had been to "grandma-sit" Tillie so Don and Ella
could go out for breakfast and have a break from
Tillie's care. Lauren thought Tillie was a sweetheart, but her memory hadn't been reliable for
years. She needed constant watching. Tillie was
likely to wander down the street, thinking it was
the 1940's and her husband was calling to her from
their barn.

Last July, Tillie had fallen and broken her hip,
making it necessary to move her to Bethany Manor
when she left the hospital. Lauren hadn't been to
visit her for a couple weeks; she might as well go
tonight.

Frowning at her dull gray sweatshirt in the mirror over her dresser, Lauren wondered if any other
seventh graders in her class were spending Friday
night visiting a nursing home for entertainment.
She bet Leesa wasn't. Something twisted in
Lauren's stomach as she recalled the way Leesa had
hung on Nick's arm and flirted with him. Lauren
knew she herself didn't stand a chance of someone
like Nick noticing her, but still . . .

Lauren shrugged, telling herself to snap out of it and go visit Tillie. Anyway, she was curious. What kind of surprise could Tillie possibly have for her?

That night after supper, Lauren bundled up and walked the three blocks to Bethany Manor nursing home. Passing the wooden windmill that turned on the lawn outside, Lauren pushed through a heavy glass door into the over-heated building. The halls were dimly lit, and a hush lay over the place. Lauren knew they ate early; supper hour was probably over in the dining halls already.

Her tennis shoes squeaked as she turned down the hallway to Room 245. Lauren sniffed in appreciation. Instead of medicine or disinfectant, the nursing home smelled of roses, even in November. Lauren sniffed again. Baby powder and hot cocoa too. If she ever had to live in a nursing home, Lauren figured this one wouldn't be too bad.

Passing the glass finch cage by the chapel, she stopped and stood beside an old man with a beaked nose. He wore a stocking cap, his gray hair hanging out of it like mop strings. Together they watched the tiny blue and gold finches flit around the enclosure. Inside, real tree branches and shrubs held tiny cup-shaped nests, lined with something that looked like cotton. In spite of her missing money, the finches' twittering songs lifted Lauren's spirits.

Down the hall and around the corner, she arrived at Tillie's room. On the door were two colorful turkeys with construction paper feathers and feet made from brown pipe cleaners. On one turkey was printed the name Tillie Nissen; the other one said Alma Jordon.

Lauren and Carl had met cranky old Alma last

spring when they tried to solve a kidnapping at the elementary school. Alma's visiting daughter, children's author Elayna Marie Hayes, had been scheduled to speak that day.

Lauren pushed open the heavy wooden door and went in. Tillie sat with her feet up in her recliner on one side of the room, her shoulders wrapped in a rainbow-striped afghan from home. On the other side of the double room, stiffly upright in a wheelchair, Alma poked through a scrap book. A few gray curls covered Alma's bony forehead above her deep-socketed eyes.

"Hi, ladies," Lauren said, letting the door softly close behind her. "Long time, no see."

"*Humph*. You're too busy with *important* things, I'm sure," Alma said, her nose in the air, "too busy to visit decrepit old ladies like us."

Lauren glanced at Tillie, whose eyes twinkled so much they looked like blue Christmas lights. Whatever she'd planned, she appeared ready to pop with it. Lauren knelt beside Tillie's chair and patted the bony knee under her robe.

"Guess what?" Tillie said, waving a hand speckled with brown spots. "I have a surprise for you."

Alma flapped the ends of her fringed shawl. "Not *her* surprise. It's *mine*."

"The suspense is killing me," Lauren said, putting a hand over her heart. "Somebody tell me quick before I go into cardiac arrest." She gave Tillie a pleading look, but Tillie was grinning at something behind Lauren.

Twisting around, Lauren spotted a coat sleeve and glove sticking out from behind the partition. As she stared, the person attached to the sleeve stepped out.

"Hello, Lauren. It's been a long time."

Lauren jumped up, tripping on her own shoes, and crashed into Tillie's bed. "Elayna!"

CHAPTER THREE

"Missing"

"I can't believe it's you!" Lauren cried.

Elayna slipped off her coat and held out her arms. "Come here. Let me hug the little gal who saved my life."

Lauren stumbled across the room, all shyness gone, and into Elayna's arms. Lauren's nose was buried in Elayna's mohair sweater, and it tickled.

"Here. Let me look at you." Elayna stood back and studied Lauren. "You've shot up at least four inches since last spring."

"You think so?" Lauren asked, stretching her neck toward the ceiling. Her below-average height was a sore point with her. Then she turned back to Tillie. "Neat surprise!"

Grinning, Tillie's hands fluttered in her lap. "We've been discussing Elayna's books."

Elayna picked up the pitcher of water on the night stand and watered the red Christmas cactus blooming on the windowsill. "I've been enjoying Tillie's stories. She's a wealth of information."

Alma bristled. She blew her nose, rubbing it till it was red. "*I* grew up here too. *I* might be a wealth of information, if you ever asked me anything."

"Of course you are, Mother," Elayna said, moving to water the ivy and philodendron. "But Tillie knew different people, so she has different stories to tell."

Hmmm . . . Lauren thought, why was Elayna collecting stories? "Are you doing research for a new book?" she asked suddenly.

Elayna disappeared into the tiny adjoining bathroom to empty the pitcher. "I can't hide much from you, can I? This town, with its historic Carousel and Grand Opera House, would make a great setting for my new novel."

"I was just at the theatre this afternoon!" Lauren said. "I'm in the *Annie, jr.* cast. Can you come next weekend?"

"I'd love to get inside the theatre again." She wrapped the gold chain she wore around and around her finger. "I haven't been in there in years."

"Are you giving a speech at the elementary school while you're back?" Lauren asked.

"Not this time. Kind of scares me to walk back into that building, after what happened last year."*

"That reminds me. There's a new elementary principal, and guess who's playing Daddy Warbucks in our musical?" Lauren asked.

"The principal?"

"Yup. And he's really good—has that big deep voice that Daddy Warbucks has in the movie. You've seen the movie, haven't you?"

"Actually, I saw it performed in New York on the stage." She stooped to mop up a pool of water that she'd spilled on the floor.

"You should come watch us rehearse tomorrow.

It's at two. I'm sure the director wouldn't mind."

Alma rolled her chair over to park right in front of Lauren. "I used to read *Little Orphan Annie* in the comics in the '30's, and she *never* sang or danced. She was too busy ducking bullets, and dodging hit-and-run cars, and blowing up submarines to run around singing."

Tillie giggled. "That's true. She was always fighting the forces of evil." She stared off into space and her voice was dreamy. "Back then, my favorite entertainment was listening to the *Lone Ranger* and *Charlie McCarthy* on the radio, and reading *Little Orphan Annie* in the comic strips."

For the first time, Alma actually smiled. "I loved *Charlie McCarthy* too," she said. "Smartest dummy I ever heard!" She laughed at her own joke. "Nothing today holds a candle to the old radio shows."

Just then Tillie fluttered a hand toward Lauren, motioning her to come closer. "I want you to buy me some of Elayna's books. I want to read them myself, and she's going to autograph them for me." Tillie pointed to her night stand. "I have money Ella gave me to spend however I want. It's hidden in my eyeglass case. The tortoise-shell one."

Elayna rummaged in the big black bag sitting with her coat. "I have a brochure in here about the theatre," she said. "I picked it up out at the mall."

"Wait. I know who you should talk to," Lauren said. She recounted Mrs. D.'s story about how Mr. Peterson got the opera house listed on the Historic Register. "She said Mr. Peterson had twenty-three notebooks *full* of neat facts about the theatre. He knew every play and movie shown at the theatre."

She took a deep breath and grinned. "And you'll never guess . . . Mr. Peterson lives here in Bethany Manor."

Elayna's eyes grew round. "Oh, how I'd love to see those notebooks. What a gold mine! I'll have to ask that nice little nurse with the ponytail where Mr. Peterson's room is. Do you suppose he'd mind a visitor?"

Alma cleared her throat with a deep, raspy *humphh*. "Remember me? I just live here. I'm nobody—not a famous writer or actress or detective or anything. I guess I'm not worth talking to." Her black eyes snapped, and her pursed lips deepened the creases around her mouth.

Lauren turned her back on the sour old woman, embarrassed for Elayna. Imagine having your own mom talk to you like that, she thought. She rummaged in Tillie's night stand, pretending she hadn't heard Alma's comments.

Pushing aside a small package of Kleenex and tiny jar of Vaseline, Lauren rooted under a pile of *Guidepost* magazines until she found Tillie's eyeglass case. She opened the case, but it was empty.

"Did you say the money was in here?" she asked, showing Tillie the empty case.

Tillie's gnarled fingers plucked nervously at the afghan around her shoulders. "I saw Ella put it in there for me just today . . ."

"Ella wasn't *here* today," Alma snapped, her voice raspy as sandpaper. "Tillie's worse than Crazy Mamie. Ella was here *yesterday* morning. She took Tillie to the dining room for lunch."

Lauren bit her tongue, but she wanted to strangle Alma, old lady or not. She had no right to snarl at Tillie or compare her to Crazy Mamie, who had shared a room with Alma before she was moved. Crazy Mamie *had* acted crazy, as Lauren recalled, imagining herself to be held hostage by Nazis. But Tillie was different. She just had confused spells, like thinking her husband, Leo, was still alive, when he'd actually been dead for years.

Tillie frowned in concentration. "But I know I saw Ella put my spending money in there. At least, I think I did . . ."

"Don't worry, Tillie," Lauren said, squatting beside her chair. "I'll ask Ella—"

"No, don't. Please." Tillie gripped Lauren's sleeve. "She already thinks I'm losing my marbles."

"Well, then, would you like to borrow my paperbacks? I have to help cater a job in the morning, but I can bring you the books after play rehearsal."

"Okay. I wish I could go to rehearsal with you," Tillie said wistfully. "When I graduated from high school, I walked across that very stage to get my diploma." She chuckled then; the hand that covered her mouth was lined with tiny blue veins. "Backstage, on the wall, I wrote the year and my name!" Her voice dropped to a guilty whisper. "Look for 'Tillie loves Leo, 1932' under the dressing room stairs." She rocked back and forth. "Wasn't I a wicked young thing to be so bold?"

"I'm totally shocked, Tillie," Lauren said, grinning.

"Well," snapped Alma, "I've done a few bold things in *my* life too, but no one's interested in me! I was never wicked though. I only had wicked people doing wicked things *to* me."

"Oh, Mother," Elayna said, "you're such a ray of

sunshine."

"I'll thank you not to mock me!" Alma spit out the words. "I'm still your mother!"

"I'm sorry," Elayna said. "I just wanted to make you laugh."

"If I wanted to laugh, I'd laugh," Alma said. "I live in a wheelchair, thanks to that accident at the Carousel. What's to laugh about that?"

Lauren leaned over and kissed Tillie on the cheek, thankful down to her toes that Alma Jordan wasn't related to *her*. But like Carl always said, you could pick your friends, but you couldn't choose your relatives.

"Here, Mother, have some chocolate. I brought your favorite kind. Maybe your blood sugar's low." Elayna passed a cut glass candy dish full of Hershey's Kisses to Tillie, Lauren and Alma.

"My blood sugar is just fine, thank *you*," Alma said, although she took three Kisses and immediately unwrapped and popped one in her mouth.

Elayna did the same. "Sweets to the sweet," she said, tossing two more to Lauren. "Say, did you know why these are called Kisses? Because the machine that makes them looks like it's kissing the conveyor belt when it squirts out the little globs of chocolate." She unwrapped a second foil-covered candy. "I read about it once."

Lauren rolled the melting chocolate around her tongue. "I should go," Lauren said reluctantly. "See you tomorrow with the books, Tillie." She waved to everyone, then hurried down the hall with a new bounce in her step. Elayna Marie Hayes was back in town! Wait till she told Carl!

On Saturday morning Carl rang the front door

bell promptly at eight o'clock. When Carousel
Catering had a job to do, they all started early.
Lauren's mom had been up at six, mixing home-
made muffins. She'd make the rosettes last, after
Lauren and Carl cut up the fruit salad.

Lauren opened the door, took Carl's winter coat
and hung it up, then nudged him toward the catering kitchen at the back of the house. Carl plopped
down on a stool at the counter. Lauren studied his
T-shirt as she edged around him.

The front pictured an eagle flying over a moun-
tain, but the back showed something gross that
looked like chopped liver. He smoothed out his shirt
so she could read it: **Eagles may fly . . . but
weasels don't get sucked into jet engines**.

"That is so gross, Carl," she said.

On the kitchen counter were four cantaloupes,
two large watermelons, a bag of red grapes, and a
fresh pineapple. "Guess who I saw last night when
I visited Tillie?" Lauren asked. She rinsed the
grapes in one side of the three-section sink, splash-
ing water on the detailed handwashing directions
posted above. "Someone is home for the holidays
and researching her newest book—"

"Elayna's in town?" Carl exclaimed.

"She's home for Thanksgiving week." Lauren
told him about her fiction book, using Story City's
historic landmarks. "She's coming to rehearsal this
afternoon."

"Really? I could tell her some great stuff about
the theatre." He popped a piece of melon in his
mouth and chewed. Juice ran down his chin.
"Remember my neighbor, Mr. Gardner? He grew up
here. He was out cleaning his gutters yesterday,

and he told me some cool stories."

Carl scooped a melon ball so enthusiastically that it popped up in the air, then fell to the floor and rolled under the refrigerator.

"Mr. Gardner remembered when the theatre had to be closed one summer because of all the weird things going on." Down on his hands and knees, Carl stretched to reach the escaped melon ball.

"What kinds of things?" Lauren asked, knife in mid-air.

"One night someone came in to clean the theatre. She swore that up on stage there were a pair of rollerskates zooming all around, doing fancy figures, but no one was in them."

"Oh, come on, you're making this up."

"Am not." Carl raised the melon ball overhead, took aim, and pitched it into the wastebasket. "And that's not all. Mr. Gardner's mother used to sell tickets for the opera, and one night she heard flute music coming from the orchestra pit, and she thought someone had come early to practice."

Lauren rolled her eyes. "Don't tell me. The flute was playing by itself too?"

"No. His mother went to tell the flute player the music was pretty, but there was no flute player. The music was floating up from under the floor."

"That's dumb."

"You might not think so if you found out later that a flute player had died the week before when she fell off the stage into the orchestra pit. Snapped her neck like a twig, Mr. Gardner said." Carl washed his hands, then sat back down with the melons. "You can laugh, but I bet Elayna would love to hear these stories. She could use them in her book."

For the next hour, while they cleaned melons and scooped out tiny melon balls, Carl and Lauren recalled the kidnapping the previous spring when they'd first met the author. "Hard to believe that was just six months ago," Lauren said.

"It'll be fun seeing her again," Carl said, glancing at the clock. "I'll finish the melon balls if you'll hack at that pineapple. I hate peeling those things."

"Okay." Lauren got a large knife from the rack by the sink, laid a cutting board on the counter, and sliced.

"Watch the knife," Carl warned. "Remember what happened to your mom on Scandinavian Days?"**

"Don't remind me. That was the worst weekend of my life."

Just as they were finishing half an hour later, Beth Burk stumbled through the front door with her arms loaded with paper bags of napkins and cups and paper plates. The next two hours passed in a flurry of loading food in the van, changing into their uniforms and hair nets, unloading food at the Doolittles' house, setting up the Christmas breads and cookies on the buffet, serving coffee and hot cider, keeping the *sandbakkels* filled with fruit, picking up dirty dishes, and refilling platters as they emptied. Lauren was surprised when she returned to the kitchen with a second tray full of dirty soup bowls and found her dad waiting.

"Time to go already?" she asked, washing her hands and grabbing a paper towel. She untied the apron that had kept her white jeans and *Carousel*

Catering T-shirt clean.

"Yup. Where's Carl?"

"Right behind you, sir." Carl clutched the big soup tureen that had been filled with *Sotsuppe*, or Sweet Soup. "I'll stick this in the van, then I'm ready to go."

Just then Beth Burk whisked into the kitchen to refill a coffee pot. "Hi, Honey," she said, grinning at her husband. "Everybody loved the Norwegian brunch. I just got two more bookings!" She gave Lauren a quick kiss. "Thanks for the help, you two. Good luck at rehearsal." With a wave, she headed to the living room to refill coffee cups.

"Let's go," Bill Burk said. "I'll drop you at the theatre, then come back and help your mom."

They were just five minutes late arriving at the theatre, and since four others were also late, Lauren and Carl slipped in without being noticed. It took a moment for Lauren's eyes to adjust to the dim interior. She suddenly pointed. "Look! Elayna's in that group by the stage door."

Dressed in jeans and a glittery Carousel sweat-shirt, Elayna sat in a front row seat surrounded by a group of kids from Lauren's class. Lauren knew they remembered Elayna from the spring before when she'd spoken at their school assembly. "I'll bet Leesa's front and center," she muttered.

She was right.

Lauren heard Leesa's nasal voice before she spotted her. "Oh, Miss Hayes! Miss Hayes!" her shrill voice squeaked. "Remember me? I was sup-posed to star in your after school special. I could still do that." Lauren watched Leesa elbow her way through the group to stand in front of the author.

"It's wonderful to see you all again," Elayna said, sticking her pencil behind her ear.

Carl pulled himself up onto the stage so he stood head and shoulders above the rest of the group. "Speaking of old friends!" he called, taking a deep bow.

"Carl, is that you?" Elayna pulled out her disposable camera and snapped his picture.

"None other!"

Leesa frowned and moved in closer. "Look, he's nobody," she said, striking a pose in her fur-trimmed velour shirt. "But I'm doing an opening solo number for *Annie, jr.* and it's something you could work into a TV special."

"I will certainly be watching," Elayna said, moving her foot back when Leesa stepped on it. She twisted around and spotted Lauren standing off to the side. "And here's the bravest girl I know."

Lauren felt the heat rising up her neck, while at the same time she was pleased at the attention. She ignored everyone's stares as she unzipped her winter coat. One arm stuck in the sleeve, and suddenly someone appeared to help her.

"Here, let me." Nick pulled her coat off, then laid it on one of the seats. "How do you know that lady?"

"It's a long story," Lauren said, crossing her arms across her catering T-shirt. Why hadn't she brought something prettier to change into? "I was just at the right place at the right time once."

"Sounded like more than that to me," he said, grinning. "You'll have to tell me—"

"Oh, Nicky! Nicky!" Leesa called. She pushed

Lauren aside as if she were invisible, then clutched Nick's arm. "You're just the muscle man I'm looking for! I need help with my props."

Embarrassed, Lauren pretended to hunt for something in her backpack. *She'd* like to help Leesa with her props, Lauren thought grimly. In fact, she wondered just how hard it would be to stuff that clown wig right down Leesa Lyon's throat.

*Carousel Mystery #1 *A Spin Out of Control*
**Carousel Mystery #2 *Deadly Disguise*

CHAPTER FOUR

"Secrets"

While Lauren pretended to hunt through her backpack, she fumed at Leesa's cooing noises as she hung on Nick's arm. What nerve she had.

"*Please*, Nicky," Leesa begged. "I need help with my tape player for my solo."

Just then Mrs. D. clapped her hands twice, loudly. "Attention, everyone." She waited till the chattering subsided. "We're going to take it from the top this afternoon. I want you to get a feel for the stage, the entrances and the exits, how the music sounds. I need the backstage crew up here now. Let's get those cots ready for the opening scene in the orphanage."

"Well, that's me," Nick said, pulling his arm away from Leesa. "Do you need help with any props?" he asked Lauren.

"Nothing I can think of—"

"Well, *I* need help with something," Leesa interrupted. "My tape player and stuffed dog are in a bag somewhere backstage and—"

"I'm afraid that's not really part of the play," Nick said, moving before she could grab his arm again. "You'll need to set that up yourself." He sidestepped her and joined a snickering Carl as they headed backstage.

Leesa's eyes narrowed to dark slits at the brush-off. Then she swung around to face Lauren. "I guess you think you're hot stuff," she hissed, her voice too low for anyone else to hear. "Well, this play would be nothing without *me*. Ms. Hayes will admit that after my performance."

Lauren stared at Leesa, wondering how she twisted her mouth into such a crooked line. She had never understood why Leesa hated her so much, or what she had ever done to her. She'd been doubly hateful ever since Lauren's best friend, Jill Cline, had landed the lead in the musical.

Jill was so quiet at school that kids and teachers sometimes forgot she was there. So when she'd auditioned for *Annie, jr.*, Lauren had been astounded at the strength of her voice and her dancing talent. Somehow, Jill's shyness had magically disappeared during tryouts, although the minute she was done, she retreated quietly to a corner again. After hearing her, no one had been surprised when she was given the lead.

Lauren couldn't wait till opening night. Jill would probably get a standing ovation. It was high time that someone besides Leesa got a leading role.

Lauren watched Leesa flounce off in a huff. She sure hoped Carl had had the good sense to hide Leesa's tape player and stuffed dog.

Up on stage, Mrs. D. walked forward to the edge and called down to Elayna. "Ms. Hayes, feel free to ask questions whenever you want. We understand you might put us in your new book?"

"Maybe. Right now I'm just taking notes, if

that's all right."

"Oh, certainly. Well, the opening scene is in Miss Hannigan's orphanage. The cots we're using are collapsible, so they won't take up much space between scenes." She jumped when Carl dropped a cot with a deafening clatter. "For some background, you might be interested to know that Little Orphan Annie was originally supposed to be a boy, Little Orphan *Otto*."

"Really?" Elayna scribbled a note.

"We're ready, Mrs. D.," Nick called out then. A row of six foldable cots were lined up on stage, as well as buckets, mops, and brooms. The backdrop showed windows looking out on a dark street.

"I need the Orphan Chorus up here now," Mrs. D. called. More than twenty boys and girls of various ages, including Lauren and Leesa, stampeded to the door beside the stage.

"What about me?" Carl asked. "Should I get my mustache on now? Mr. Bundles comes early in the story."

Lauren waited with the others in the wings. She spotted Nick watching her, and she felt the dreaded heat climbing up her neck. Would she *ever* outgrow blushing? She turned and pretended to be interested in Carl's role as the mustached laundry man, Mr. Bundles.

"No mustaches or beards or anything today," Mrs. D. said. "We'll save that for next week when our Makeup Moms are here. For now, just use your imagination for costumes and makeup."

With clattering feet and chattering mouths, the Orphan Chorus moved into place, ready to sing "Hard-Knock Life" while the gymnasts did their tumbling routine with the mops and buckets. But first, Jill would sing the opening number, "Maybe." Lauren tried to ignore Leesa's glares as they lined up beside each other in the wings.

Mrs. D. raised her arms for attention. "Don't forget, chorus members, the key to good vocal projection lies in proper vocal support and vocal placement." She turned where Jill waited center stage to do her first solo. "And Jill, remember to breathe from your diaphragm."

"Good luck, Lauren," Nick said, touching her arm. Then, ignoring Leesa, he walked through the group to perch on the steps leading up to the dressing room.

That was apparently the last straw. In high clear tones, Leesa called out to the director, "Mrs. D., I think we should do the play *Little Orphan Otto* instead."

Mrs. D. looked very annoyed. "What, Leesa?"

"Yes, and I know who should play the lead too." She threw a spiteful look at Lauren first, then over her shoulder at Nick, but her voice was surgary sweet. "We have an orphan right here with us, someone who could truly play the part of the child nobody wants. Isn't that right, *Nick?*"

Lauren blinked in confusion. What was Leesa babbling about? She was acting like a cobra Lauren had once seen on TV, mesmerizing her victim, then suddenly spitting poison.

Nick's face flushed a dull brick red, and he clenched and unclenched his fists held stiffly against his sides.

Leesa's voice cut through the strained silence. "Here's Nick, starring as himself in *Little Orphan*

Otto." She laughed aloud.

Suddenly Nick exploded. "Take that back!" He advanced toward Leesa, but Carl grabbed his arm. Nick dragged Carl along with him as if he weighed nothing. "I'm no orphan."

"Ha. My mother said your dad deserted you and your mom's as good as dead."

Nick's voice broke, and he winced as if he'd been struck. Lauren's throat burned when she saw the tears in his eyes. "My mom's not dying. She's *not*."

"Children! That's enough." Mrs. D.'s sharp voice sliced through the air like a knife. "Leesa, not another word."

"Sorry, Mrs. D." Leesa smiled smugly at Lauren, then turned innocent eyes on the play director. "I didn't mean to upset him."

Oh, sure, Lauren thought, getting back in place. Her heart sank as she watched Nick shove Carl aside and disappear around the edge of the beige curtain. What had that been all about? Was his mother really dying? If only Lauren could help, but how? *Obviously,* she realized, *Annie isn't the only one who's had a hard-knock life.*

CHAPTER FIVE

"Lady in Black"

No matter how hard she tried, Lauren couldn't keep her mind focused on "Hard-Knock Life," and she kept singing in the wrong places. Where was Nick? Was he okay? And what in the world had Leesa meant about his mother? Finally the song was over, and Lauren collapsed to the floor.

At least Jill Cline was fabulous as Annie. The wistful song "Maybe" wouldn't leave a dry eye in the house, Mrs. D. said. Jill's talent had been a terrific and welcome surprise to them all. Well, Lauren corrected herself, welcome to everyone except Leesa, who'd expected to walk away with the lead.

Out of the corner of her eye, Lauren watched Leesa. Eyebrows bunched together, her scowl withered anyone who dared to glance her way. As Jill finished the high notes of "Maybe," Leesa's jealousy was obvious in the narrowed eyes and her sneering lips. Except Leesa wasn't green with envy, Lauren noticed. Her face was a blotchy purple instead. After that attack on Nick, Lauren was glad that Leesa was miserable.

A deafening *crash* behind Lauren made her jump and whirl around. Six cots had been lined up across the stage, but now the one on the far end had collapsed. Buckled in half, it was wrapped around Sadie Anne, the smallest orphan in the group.

"Let me out!" she screamed. "Somebody help me!"

Jill's song ended abruptly. Mr. Blue, the stage manager, dressed in paint-splattered overalls and cap, rushed forward. Carl reached her first and pulled open the canvas cot so Sadie Anne could crawl out. "Are you okay?" he asked.

The slender blonde rubbed her right elbow, which Lauren could see was scraped raw. "Man, this really throbs," Sadie Anne said. She moved her arm slowly and winced. "Look. There's a fat bump on the side already."

Mr. Blue shook his big shaggy head, reminding Lauren of an old lion.   "How'd this happen?"

"I don't know," Carl said. "I braced the legs."

"You *have* to be careful." Mr. Blue squatted beside the collapsed cot, muttering under his breath, "You young kids have no business using this theatre."

Lauren glanced up just then and happened to catch a smug expression on Leesa's face before she stomped off into the wings. Leesa actually looked happy about the accident. Lauren frowned. Could Leesa have unhooked the brace on the cot? She'd been standing on that end of the stage during the last song. It would have been simple to step back, kick the brace loose, then rejoin the chorus. But why, Lauren wondered, would she do a thing like that?

Elayna leaned on the edge of the stage. "Can I get Sadie Anne some ice for her elbow? There's ice in the concession room, I bet."

"Oh, thank you," Mrs. D. said. "Sadie Anne? Go with Ms. Hayes and put some ice on that swelling right away."

Holding her arm, Sadie Anne trotted up the aisle with the author in search of an ice pack. Lauren sat down again and waited. The tall, thin stage manager double-checked that the legs of all six beds were locked.

"There," Mr. Blue said, looking around the stage area. The angles of his face were sharp. "Let's not be having any more accidents. Carl, pick up that coil of rope on the floor. Hang it on the nail under the stairs there. And that wrench goes downstairs on the tool bench." Mr. Blue sat on each cot himself to make sure they were stable.

Carl picked up the rope and wrench, hung the rope on a nail, then disappeared downstairs for a minute. He returned empty-handed and plopped down next to Lauren while Mrs. D. blocked out the next song, "Little Girls."

Lauren told him about Leesa's smug look after the cot collapsed. "That was dumb, if she did it," Lauren said. "It just stopped the rehearsal. We need all the practicing we can get."

"I bet that creepy Leesa would rather see the play flop than let Jill look more important than her."

"That doesn't make sense," Lauren said. "If the play flops, Leesa will look bad right along with the rest of us."

"Not if she gets to do her solo routine first. I bet nothing would make her happier than to have her brilliant solo be followed by a play that stinks."

Lauren's smile tightened, and she had to agree. "I can just hear her now. *'If they'd only given ME the part of Annie, I could have saved the show!'*"

Just then Mrs. D. clapped her hands. "Okay, kids, until Sadie Anne gets back, I want it quiet for the solo. I think Jill's ready to run through it."

Hands clasped in front of her, Jill moved to center stage where Mrs. D. had marked with masking tape, then waited for the CD music. Miss Roberts, one of the co-producers, clicked through the sound track of the accompaniment and after some scene change music, she found the music for "Little Girls."

Sitting Indian-style, Lauren leaned back on her hands and listened as Jill sang. A grin slowly spread across Lauren's face. Jill was really good. She must have practiced dozens of hours at home because now she sounded just like Annie in the movie.

Halfway through the song, the music swelled and Jill threw her arms overhead, twirled, and turned to race across the stage. Suddenly the floodlights overhead flared twice as bright, nearly blinding Lauren. She shaded her eyes against the glare. Jill stopped halfway across the stage, did some fancy dance steps and a back flip, then continued the rest of the way across. Lauren wondered how she could see anything the way those lights glared.

Lauren watched her friend, grinning at her high energy performance, but the grin suddenly froze on her face. She spotted it the same instant Mrs. D. did, and they shouted together, "Jill! Look out!"

Jill looked up in confusion just as her right foot caught the coil of rope. It tangled her feet, and she slipped, then couldn't regain her footing. She fell hard, her ankle bent beneath her at an odd angle. She lay there, moaning.

Lauren scrambled to her feet and rushed forward. Mrs. D. got to Jill at the same time.

"*Carl!*" Mr. Blue's voice roared above the dance music that continued to play. "*I told you to pick up that rope!*"

Carl, for the first time since Lauren had known him, was speechless. "I-I-I, uh . . ." His voice trailed off helplessly as he stared at the back wall where he'd hung the coil of rope not ten minutes earlier. The nail was empty now. "But I did pick it up."

Lauren glanced around quickly, half expecting to see Leesa in the wings. Shading her eyes, she wished someone in the light booth would turn down the floodlights that hung overhead. Lauren finally spotted Leesa down below in the front row of seats, studying her script as if nothing unusual had happened onstage.

Lauren backed away from Jill as Mrs. D. examined her ankle. "I saw you pick up the rope," Lauren told Carl when she joined him. "I guess someone knocked it off the nail somehow."

"Oh, sure. And accidentally threw it back onstage where somebody would trip?" Carl's eyes narrowed to tiny slits. "I'm starting to wonder about those weird spook stories about this old theatre. We seem jinxed."

Just then Elayna and Sadie Anne came down the aisle to the front of the stage. Sadie Anne held a plastic bag of ice cubes against her elbow.

"Oh, dear. Need more ice?" Elayna called.

Mrs. D. nodded grimly. "I'm afraid ice, plus at least 24 hours off this ankle." She sighed, closed her eyes for a minute, then raised her voice. "Rehearsal's over for today. I think we understand better now how careful we all need to be. We'll practice again Monday after school, and I'm sure things will go much better then."

She called Miss Roberts to help Jill down off the stage, but Nick appeared out of nowhere. "Here. Let me help." He avoided meeting the director's eye. "We've got to take care of the star of the show." He lifted Jill easily, and Lauren felt a twinge of envy that Nick was carrying her friend. He set Jill gently in a front row seat.

"Thanks, Nick." Mrs. D. turned to the rest of the group. "Be sure to gather up all your things down in the seats. Take it all home with you. Todd needs to lower the screen now for tonight's movie." She called down to Nick. "By the way, the posters you put up around town look great. Thanks so much for helping."

"No problem." Nick rubbed a hand over his curly hair, which flattened and sprung back magically into place. "I can hand out programs before performances too, if you want. Or take tickets, or seat people."

"We'll take all the help you want to give," Mrs. D. said, the first real smile on her face all afternoon.

Lauren turned to look for Carl, but was surprised at the dark scowl on his face. "Come on, Mr. Bundles, don't look so grim." Lauren crossed her eyes at him, but he didn't crack a smile. "The accident wasn't your fault. I know you hung up the rope; I saw you."

"Tell it to Mr. Blue. Did you hear him bark at me?" He jammed his fists into his pockets. "I'll keep my eyes peeled from now on. *Nothing* and *nobody's* going to jinx this play, then put the blame on me."

They were outside the theatre before Lauren remembered her song book. "I have to go back and get it," she said.

The theatre was empty when Lauren hurried back inside, but she could hear adult voices backstage somewhere. She checked the row of seats where she'd laid her coat, but there was no sign of her song book. Maybe somebody had picked it up. She turned to leave, then spotted it down under the seat.

Down on hands and knees between the rows of red plastic-covered seats, Lauren reached for her song book. Just then Mrs. D. and Miss Roberts emerged from backstage. Lauren started to call out, but something in Mrs. D.'s voice made her hesitate.

". . . but we can't be spreading rumors," Mrs. D. said. "We want the kids to enjoy theatre and have it be an enriching experience."

"If you call twisting your ankle and being eaten by a cot an enriching experience," Miss Roberts replied.

"Accidents happen," Mrs. D. said tiredly, "but we can't let the older boys tell the little ones there's a ghost loose in here."

Miss Roberts' voice dropped to a hush that Lauren could barely hear. "Um, just between you and me, you don't believe those stories, do you? You know, about the phantom and everything."

"Oh, not you too."

"I didn't say *I* believed anything," Miss Roberts

said. "But have you heard what happened in here just last weekend?"

Footsteps crossed the stage, and Lauren heard the two women come down the steps to the audience level. Lauren held her breath and buried her face in her hands. She knew she ought to stand up and be seen, but it was too late now. She closed her eyes and prayed that they wouldn't see her.

"Well, what happened?" Mrs. D. asked, her voice tired.

"Late last Wednesday night, someone passed by the theatre and saw a woman in the lobby. She was dressed in black with a cape, and she was wearing a 1900's style hat. Very elegant."

"Who was it?"

"That's just it. No one knows." Miss Roberts' voice rose excitedly. "She carried opera glasses and a program."

"Are you saying this woman in black was a phantom?" Mrs. D. burst out laughing.

"Well, that's not all," Miss Roberts said. "Someone called Todd that very same night and asked what was going on in the theatre because they could hear a man singing opera music. Todd came down, but the theatre was empty."

Mrs. D. sighed. "Where do these stories get started? Let's go home and give our opera singer and Lady in Black all the space they need."

Miss Roberts laughed too. "You have to admit, this would be the perfect place for a few ghosts to hang out. Can't you imagine them floating up in the balcony together, or strolling the catwalk?"

Both ladies laughed at that. Lauren ducked her head down as they passed by the end of her row.

Their voices faded out as they moved on up the aisle to the lobby. Lauren waited till she heard the front lobby door *whoosh* shut, then she scrambled to her feet. Pausing for just a second, she decided to leave out the side EXIT door. She'd go home by way of the back alley, and no one would ever know she'd gone back in the theatre.

At the EXIT door, with her hand on the bar to push it open, she turned and glanced at the stage. The curtain rustled, then settled back into place. A shiver ran down Lauren's spine. Was someone still back there? She didn't hear anything. Probably just a cold draft blowing through a crack some-where.

Or the ghostly opera singer waiting for the Lady in Black, Lauren thought, pushing the door open and stepping outside into the frigid November air.

CHAPTER SIX

"Bah! Humbug!"

Lauren blinked in the chilly afternoon sunshine, jumped down off the cement step, and let the EXIT door close behind her. Relieved at her escape, she turned toward the alley.

A giggle behind her made Lauren whip around, but she saw no one. *What the heck?*

A movement on the fire escape caught her eye just before she was hit in the face by a huge fuzzy lump. Lauren staggered back, staring at the stuffed dog at her feet. Then she glanced upward. At the top of the fire escape, Leesa broke out laughing, then clattered down the stairs.

"Surprised you, didn't I?" she asked, picking up the one-eyed Sandy.

Lauren glanced from Leesa to the fire escape door at the top of the stairs. She knew that door led to the theatre balcony. "What were you doing up in the balcony just now?" she demanded.

"Ha! The *real* question is, why were *you* hiding down in the seats and eavesdropping on Mrs. D.?"

Lauren gasped. "I wasn't eavesdropping. I forgot my song book and it fell under the seat—"

"Save your breath." Leesa socked Lauren in the

arm with the stuffed Sandy. "I saw you hiding and listening the whole time Miss Roberts and Mrs. D. were talking about that stupid opera ghost. Then you snuck out the side door."

Lauren bent her head into the wind. What could she say? Leesa was right. She *had* eavesdropped, but that hadn't been the reason she was down between the seats.

Lauren glanced sideways at Leesa as they fell into step in the gravel alley. Leesa's ear muffs were a perfect match with her lavender coat and mittens, their brand new condition a real contrast to the scroungy dog. What *had* Leesa been doing up by the lights and sound booths just now? She hadn't answered Lauren's question.

Suddenly Lauren recalled the night before, when the lights had gone out and she'd heard footsteps overhead in the balcony. *Someone* had messed with the lights. Had he or she then disappeared out the fire escape door too?

". . . makes perfect sense to me," Leesa said.

Lauren stumbled, scattering gravel ahead of her. "What did you say?"

"Pay attention." Leesa swung the dog at Lauren again, but this time Lauren saw it coming and ducked. "I *said* this ghost junk must be Mrs. D.'s idea. I bet she's spreading the rumors."

That's stupid, Lauren thought. "Why would she do that?" she asked aloud. "It messes up rehearsals."

"I'll tell you why she's doing this," Leesa said. "My mom told my dad that Mrs. D. paid some music theatre outfit in California too much money for the rights to *Annie, jr.* So they've got to draw a bigger crowd than usual to cover the costs."

"By telling ghost stories?" Lauren asked. "Get real."

"What better way to make people curious and boost sales than to have mysterious happenings take place in the theatre?"

"Are you nuts?" Lauren asked, staying well out of reach of the moth-eaten mutt. "Mrs. D. would never do that."

"Think about it, Brainless." Leesa tossed her blonde hair over her shoulder, but the wind promptly blew it back in her face. "It makes perfect sense."

What made perfect sense to Lauren, however, was that Leesa was so mad at the director for not giving her the part of Annie that Leesa *herself* was causing the accidents and interrupting the rehearsals. Lauren bet Leesa was selfish enough to do it too. If she couldn't be the star, nobody else was going to be. However, Lauren kept her opinion to herself. She was tired of being whacked by that one-eyed dog.

When Lauren got home, the Carousel Catering van was back from the brunch and parked in the driveway. Inside, the kitchen was already spotless. "Shhh," her dad said when he leaned around the doorway of his office, "your mom's napping."

Lauren tugged on her lower lip for a moment. She'd promised those books to Tillie. Now would be a good time to take them to her.

"Tell Mom I went to see Tillie, okay?" Lauren zipped her coat back up, jammed on a knitted hat, grabbed her books from the shelf, and headed back outside, careful to shut the front door quietly.

But when she arrived at Tillie's and Alma's

room, it was empty. Lauren frowned. It was only
4:35. Where could they be?

She stood in the doorway for ten minutes, shift-
ing from one foot to the other in impatience. Even
the nurses' station, decorated with ceramic Pilgrim
figures, was deserted. In fact, the hall was empty
except for a lady mopping the floor. Lauren fanned
herself with her mitten, wondering why it was
always so hot in the nursing home.

Finally Lauren wandered in the direction of the
chapel, planning to peek in there before checking
out the multipurpose room. But as she approached
the dining area, the aroma of roast turkey and
pumpkin pie made her realize that the evening
meal was already being served.

At the dining room door, Lauren tried to spot
Tillie in the sea of gray curls and bald heads.
Residents ate at small tables, in groups of three or
four. Each table held a Thanksgiving centerpiece,
and the walls were decorated with construction
paper turkeys and colored autumn leaves. Lauren
smiled as she realized how dressed up everyone
was, the men in knit shirts and sweaters, and ladies
wearing earrings and necklaces.

Lauren finally spotted Tillie at a table with an
old man and Alma, and they already had their
dessert. Tiny blobs of whipped cream sat atop each
piece of pumpkin pie. Alma's pie was half gone, but
Tillie's was untouched. She slumped at the table,
head in her hand. The man, stocky and broad-
shouldered, looked worried as he stroked his mustache.

Lauren walked quietly up behind the trio and
heard Alma's sharp voice cutting through the sur-

rounding chatter. "Stop blubbering, Tillie. You're loony. You'd lose your head if it wasn't screwed on."

The old man shook his nearly bald head at Alma. "You keep your opinions to yourself," he advised.

"You deaf old coot," Alma snapped. "She's a dim bulb." She stuffed another piece of pie in her mouth and talked while she chewed. "A nicer one than Crazy Mamie, I admit, but not the brightest bulb on the Christmas tree, if you get my meaning." She reached across to Tillie's untouched pie. "I'll eat this if you're not going to."

Teeth clenched, Lauren stepped up and gently laid both hands on Tillie's shoulders. "Tillie's no crazier than I am," she said, scowling at Alma. "You shouldn't talk like that." *How* did that nice author lady have such a nasty woman for a mother?

Alma laughed, but it sounded more like a bark. She kept eating.

Tillie glanced around as she wiped her watery eyes on her Thanksgiving napkin. "Oh, Lauren, I'm glad you came. I don't know what to do!"

"What's happened?"

"My diamond ring from Leo is missing! I left it on my night stand before breakfast, and when I got back, it was gone."

"Someone stole it?" A nagging voice in the back of Lauren's head reminded her that Shawn had worked the breakfast shift that morning. *Why* was Shawn always around when something bad happened?

Alma licked her finger, then jabbed the crumbs on her plate to pick them up. "Nothing was stolen," she snapped. "Tillie's losing her mind, that's all."

Lauren glared at Alma, who ignored her.

However, Lauren was afraid that Alma might be partly right. Tillie was getting more and more forgetful. Often her valuables turned up in odd places: money under her pillow, a watch in a sweater pocket, postage stamps in a vase of flowers once. Lauren's heart ached for Tillie—it must be hard to get so forgetful, to realize your mind had a few leaks in it.

"Can you hunt for my ring?" Tillie asked, gripping Lauren's hand with surprising strength.

"I can whenever you go back to your room." Lauren pulled up an extra chair beside Tillie, squeezing in between the two women. Alma glared at her, but moved to make room. The man at the next table looked up briefly, his right hand gripping his fork. He belched, grinned at Lauren, then stretched his mouth around another huge forkful of food.

Tillie dipped the tea bag in her cup up and down as she said, "Lauren, this is Henry." Tillie patted the elderly man's arm. "Henry, tell Lauren what you just told us."

"What's that?" Henry asked.

"Tell Lauren about your pocket watch!"

"What about your watch?" Lauren asked. Henry didn't reply. Lauren noticed his hearing aid and leaned forward so he could read her lips. "What about your pocket watch?" she repeated.

Henry patted his pants pocket. "I carry my watch here, but two days ago it turned up missing."

"Stolen?"

"I hate to think so." Henry wrapped his gnarled hands around his half-empty coffee mug. He blew on his coffee, but he didn't drink it. "My son gave me that watch for Christmas six years ago."

Alma swallowed a huge bite of pie, leaving whipped cream in the corners of her mouth. "You're both cuckoo," she said, waving her fork through the air. A piece of pumpkin flew onto Lauren's shirt front. "You couldn't find your own rooms if they took down those stupid turkeys on the doors."

Henry fiddled with his hearing aid, and Lauren bet he was tuning Alma out. She didn't blame him. She wished Tillie could do the same thing. At the next table, the man belched again, but stayed bent over his plate, rapidly shoveling food into his mouth.

"You're both soft in the head too," Alma said. "Giving money to every Tom, Dick and Harry that feeds you a sob story."

Tillie pursed her lips and drew herself up straight. "Giving to worthy causes is *not* falling for sob stories," Tillie said. "It's Thanksgiving. We *should* share with others at this time of year."

"Oh, forget it!" Alma took a last slurp of tea, then shoved hard against the table, pushing her wheelchair away. Two apples were jarred loose from the cornucopia centerpiece and rolled across the table. "I'm going back to my room to wait for my long lost daughter to show up. You old geezers wear me out."

Silence settled over the table after she rolled away. Then Tillie smiled. "That's what I love about Alma. Such a boost to one's spirits."

Lauren giggled, replacing the apples in the cornucopia. "Have you both reported your missing ring and watch?" she asked.

"I told that nice young nurse," Tillie said, "but

she didn't believe me. I could tell."

Henry rested his elbows on the table, made a teepee with his hands, and rested his chin on the tips of his fingers. Then he shifted and stared down into his coffee mug as he stirred around and around.

"Henry?" Lauren touched his arm.

He looked up then, his eyes watery. He twisted a dial on his hearing aid.

Lauren asked again, "Did you tell anyone your watch was missing?"

Henry slowly shook his head. "People think you're loony when you talk like that. Then you lose what little freedom you have left."

"But it's not right to keep quiet if there's a thief on the loose," Lauren said. *Oh, please, don't let it be Shawn*, she pleaded silently, suddenly remembering his recent car repair bills. Was *that* where he'd found the money to fix his jalopy?

Lauren jumped as a plate was dropped just behind her. She glanced over her shoulder to see pumpkin pie upside down on the tile floor, and a plate smashed in four pieces. A fork skidded across the polished floor. A high school girl in white jeans and an apron came running with a dishpan and paper towels.

At their table Lauren stacked the dirty pie plates and brushed crust crumbs into a little pile. "What was Alma talking about a minute ago? Something about giving to charity?"

"You remember my nurse, Jenny?" Tillie asked.

Lauren nodded.

"Well, her brother's in the Army, and he visited her this week. He's home on leave for

Thanksgiving." She smiled dreamily, a far-off look in her eyes. "He looked so much like my son, Don, when he was in the service. I do love a man in uniform."

Henry grinned. One of his front teeth was rimmed in gold, like a picture frame. "Ahh, the good old days," he agreed. "Of course, it's hard for our servicemen to be away from their families at the holidays."

Tillie hugged herself, as if suddenly chilly. "Jenny's brother's stationed in Germany, don't you know. He'll be there over Christmas this year, like most of the young men."

Henry placed his fingertips together, tapping them lightly. "Yes, we gave him money to buy a few Christmas gifts for our boys overseas," he said proudly. "It's such a small thing to do, really."

"That's right," Tillie agreed. "And Bobby—that's Jenny's brother—said there were orphans living under bridges over there, without warm clothes or enough food. We gave him some money for them too. He said his friends would spend Christmas with the orphans and take them food and some coats and mittens." Her face glowed as she talked about it. "That makes me really happy, giving like that, especially at the holidays."

Lauren nodded, wondering if that's where Tillie's money had gone, the money that Ella had hidden in her eyeglass case. "My mom says the same thing about working at the Food Pantry," Lauren said. "She says we forget about the tough times people go through."

"I used to help at Loaves and Fishes Food Pantry," Henry said. "We donated to that last week too."

"Really? Where'd you get cans of food?"

"We didn't give food, just a little money." Henry
scooted back from the table and stood, gripping the
edge of the table with one hand and reaching for the
cane that hung on the back of his chair with the
other. "A boy collected money last week. Said they
were buying turkeys for the Thanksgiving baskets
this year."

"Are you sure?" Lauren asked, surprised. "Mom
didn't mention that."

"That poor boy taking donations had such a bad
limp," Tillie said, "and his glasses were thicker than
mine. Poor boy," she said again.

Lauren helped Tillie to her feet, wondering why
the nursing home staff allowed people in to ask the
residents for donations. It was generous of the
elderly people to give, but when their memories
were as foggy as Tillie's, she had to wonder if it was
a good idea. She bet Ella had no idea that Tillie was
giving away the money she left for her.

Following behind Tillie, Lauren realized with a
sinking feeling that the old woman had shrunk. It
was clear from the way her clothing hung that she'd
dropped close to twenty pounds since she broke her
hip. On the way back to her room, they left Henry
in the chapel. He said a Christmas piano recital
was scheduled in half an hour and he wanted a
front row seat. Near the nurses' station, Jenny
whisked around the corner, her stethoscope swinging.

"How was supper?" she asked Tillie. "I could
smell that turkey and stuffing clear down here!"

"Quite good. Not like Ella's, but very adequate."

Tillie leaned heavily on Lauren's arm. "We were just discussing your brother, Bobby. My, he cuts a dashing figure in his uniform."

"He does. That's a fact." Jenny beamed. "He's still my baby brother, though, even if he's in the Army."

"How long is he home?" Lauren asked.

"Till the Saturday after Thanksgiving."

"I wish he'd come back to visit," Tillie said wistfully. "We had such a nice talk."

"Did you? I didn't know that." Jenny popped a mint in her mouth. "I'll tell him to stop in and see you when he comes back." She disappeared into a nearby linen closet.

Lauren helped Tillie to her room, then came back out in the hallway to wait. She wanted to ask the nurse about Tillie's ring. Soon the nurse reappeared, her arms piled high with white fluffy towels. Jenny reached for a clipboard on the cart and checked off several items on a list.

She glanced up and smiled. "Everybody loves my brother, Bobby. It was so typical of him to visit some elderly ladies he doesn't even know." She reached into her pocket for a small leather photo album. "I have a picture of him here. Would you like to see it?"

She flipped through several photos, then slid one out of its plastic covering and handed it to Lauren. The boy in the picture wasn't much older than Shawn, maybe early twenties, but very serious in his Army uniform. His eyes were a very light clear blue. Lauren could understand why he'd made such an impression on Tillie, even if his hair was nearly shaved off.

"He looks really nice," Lauren said, handing back the picture. "I was wondering—"

The nurse's beeper went off then, and she listened, then rushed off down the hall. When Lauren returned to Tillie's room, Alma the Scrooge was waiting.

"I heard what you said to that nurse," Alma snapped. "I don't want that soldier in this room, do you hear me? He'll steal us blind with his sob stories about freezing orphans." She gripped the sides of her wheelchair with fingers that curved like claws. "Did you notice his boots? Looked more like high heels!"

Tillie settled back into her rocking chair while Lauren spread an afghan over her knees. "Didn't you ever see a pair of Army boots?" Tillie shook her head. "Don't worry, dear. I'm sure that handsome soldier is much too busy to spend his time visiting old ladies." She lowered her voice and turned to Lauren. "Especially such *crabby* old ladies," she whispered.

"I heard that," Alma said. "Bah! Humbug!"

Lauren couldn't help it. She burst out laughing.

CHAPTER SEVEN

"Accident"

First thing Monday morning, after attendance was taken in home room, Lauren hurried to the principal's office to report her missing money. In the office, she waited behind a boy buying a pencil and a girl turning in a pair of gloves to the Lost and Found.

"Next?" said the secretary, Mrs. Baker. Her hazel eyes peered at Lauren over a pair of half-glasses which she wore low on her nose. "What can I do for you, Lauren?"

"I had some money stolen at lunch last Friday."

"Oh, dear, I'm sorry." Mrs. Baker rubbed her very red nose and reached for a notepad and pencil. "How much money?"

"Fifty dollars." Self-consciously, Lauren smoothed down her brightly colored sweater, still like new, a gift from her aunt last Christmas. It felt funny not wearing her usual gray T-shirt or sweatshirt. She hoped Nick would like it—she thought the sweater made her look older. Lauren sighed. Who was she kidding? Would Nick even notice?

Mrs. Baker sneezed, blew her nose, then wrote down the number. "Fifty dollars is a lot of money to be carrying in school."

"I know, but I was going to the bank right after play rehearsal. There wasn't time to go home for it."

Mrs. Baker sniffled. "Was your locker left unlocked at lunch time?"

"I didn't put it in my locker. I hid it in the bottom of my backpack, and I wore it all day." Lauren leaned her arms on top of the long counter. "I only took the backpack off to save my seat while I got my spaghetti."

"I hate hearing this." Mrs. Baker tapped the pencil eraser against her front tooth. "So far thefts haven't been a problem this year."

Lauren heard the office door open and close behind her. "What should I do now?" she asked, tugging at the itchy white turtleneck shirt under her sweater. "The money was for Christmas presents."

"I'll tell the principal when he finishes his meeting. He may want to talk to you. In the meantime, go back to class."

"Okay." Lauren pivoted on her heel and rammed into Leesa.

"Watch it," Leesa snapped, glancing at Lauren's sweater. "My! Don't we look fancy today? And *whom* are we trying to impress?" Leesa arched one eyebrow, but then looked quickly away.

Lauren's face burned. Leesa had guessed—correctly—that she'd dressed up today for Nick. Maybe she should change back into the sweatshirt in her book bag. Lauren glanced sideways when Leesa sniffled. Her eyes were sure red. Lauren edged around Leesa toward the door.

"Yes, Leesa?" Mrs. Baker said, violently sneezing twice.

"I, uh, I'm late," she mumbled. "I don't have a note."

Mrs. Baker reached for another Kleenex. "That's the third time this month, dear. You need to make an effort to be on time."

"I *do* try."

Lauren knelt down to tie her trailing shoe laces, surprised that the perfect Leesa had a tardy record.

"What happened this time?" Mrs. Baker said, reaching for the yellow pad of school passes. Nose in the air, she stared down through her half-glasses. "What reason shall I write?"

"Um, just a family emergency." Leesa turned and glared at Lauren. "Do you mind?"

Lauren quickly finished tying her shoe and left. As the door was closing behind her, Lauren heard Leesa add, "I was waiting for my dad. He and my mom, well—" And the door clicked shut. Puzzled, Lauren raced back to home room.

That day after school, the rehearsal at the theatre started promptly at four o'clock. "Gather around, kids," Mrs. D. said, emerging onstage from the wings. "We have a lot of ground to cover. I hope you're well rested after the weekend."

Shrieks and giggles erupted from a group of five kids sitting on the edge of the stage, but Mrs. D.'s warning smile silenced them. She moved center stage where everyone could see her.

"We'll start with the opening scene again. Props boys, get the cots set up." She flipped pages on her clipboard. "We'll run through 'Maybe' first, then 'Hard-Knock Life.' Jill, you just sing today and skip the handsprings. Let's give that ankle one more day of rest. Just four days till Opening Night, kids!" She paced back and forth as she flipped pages of her script. "If time permits, we'll do the scene where Annie hides in Mr. Bundles' laundry basket."

"Mrs. D.!" Leesa waved her hand wildly. "Should I do my introduction first?" She jumped up. "My mom bought me a better costume over the weekend. It's just like Annie's red dress, only fancier." She smirked at Jill. "I bought a new dog too— he's got a red scarf and little red doggy sweater."

Carl snickered and poked Lauren. "Not that again." Carl called above the groans of the group. "Give it up!"

"You want the audience to hurl before the curtain even goes up?" Mark, one of the Orphan Chorus, asked.

"Oh, shut up." Leesa turned back to the director, worked her dimples and batted her long eyelashes. "I practiced my routine all weekend. Now sets exactly the right tone for the musical." She dimpled then in Nick's direction, but Lauren noticed that he quickly stared at the backdrop scenery. Lauren hoped he was still mad about Leesa calling him an unwanted orphan.

Mrs. D. held her script in her teeth, then pulled her hair up and pinned it on top of her head. "If there's time today *after* we cover everything on my rehearsal schedule, you can do your routine." She clapped her hands again. "But first, places, everybody. Nick, lower the backdrop we need. Carl, get those cots up, and be sure the legs are locked this time."

Carl saluted. The group of orphans hustled up

the steps to the stage. Mrs. D. tapped Lauren's arm as she went by. "Could you do me a favor?" she asked.

"Sure. What?"

"Up in the King Kong dressing room—you remember which one that is?" At Lauren's nod, she said, "I left some makeup supplies up there in a lavender carrying case. Carl's mustache is in it. Also the white laundry man's jacket for Mr. Bundles is hanging on the rack too. Could you get them for me?"

"No problem."

Up on stage, Lauren scooted along the row of colored footlights near the front. In the wings, she pushed through a chattering cluster of third grade orphans to the dressing room stairs. Grasping the railing, she started up to the King Kong dressing room.

Halfway up, she became aware of voices floating somewhere above and behind her. What in the world?

Hanging onto the railing, she turned around and craned her neck upward. On the catwalk overhead were the forms of two people, half hidden by the catwalk itself. She peered up into the shadows and strained to hear. She recognized their voices even before her eyes adjusted to the dimness: Nick and Leesa.

Good grief, Lauren thought. What was Leesa doing up there? Had Nick invited her up there? Lauren's stomach flipflopped at the idea.

Lauren knew that Nick's main job was to raise and lower the backdrops for different scenes in the play. His strong wrestler's arms were put to good use on those ropes. But Leesa had no business being on the catwalk. Standing perfectly still just below them out of sight, Lauren listened hard to hear over the noise of the cots being set up.

". . . really, it's not a big deal." Nick's voice was gruff. "Just don't bring it up again."

"But I'm really so very, very *sorry*," Leesa pleaded. "I was feeling attacked about my dance routine, but I never should have said that about your mother."

A hard edge crept into Nick's voice, but his words were calm and slow. "Like I said, it's forgotten."

"Oh, Nicky, is it really?" Leesa crooned.

Oh, barf, Lauren thought. Overhead, two sets of footsteps shuffled back and forth. It sounded to Lauren like Nick was testing various ropes while Leesa moved along with him, like an attached Siamese twin.

"You'd better move before I bump into you," Nick said. "In fact, maybe you should climb down. Nobody but Mr. Blue or me is supposed to be up on the catwalk."

"I'll go in a minute." Leesa's voice was drowned out briefly by a blare of music from the CD. "—go out after Opening Night with me, maybe out to dinner or a late show in Ames?"

Lauren's eyes nearly bugged out of her head. Leesa Lyons, a lowly seventh grader, was asking a high school boy out of a *date*? Lauren held her breath.

Lauren could tell by Nick's voice that he was dying to laugh. "Um, well, gee, that's um, real nice of you." He shuffled a few steps away from her. "But I've got plans."

"Can't you change them?" Leesa whined.

"I don't think it would be a good idea," Nick said.

"Why?"

There was a long pause, and Lauren held her breath. Mrs. D. was waiting for that costume and makeup case but Lauren was frozen in place on the stairs. *Come on, come on, answer her,* she thought.

A backdrop of a 1920's street scene with brick house fronts and painted-on flower boxes of geraniums was slowly lowered as Nick answered. "You're a cute kid, Leesa," he finally said, "but you're what? Eleven?"

"I'm *twelve,* and I'll be a *teenager* before Christmas."

"Still, I'm fifteen. It'd be like dating somebody's baby sister."

"I'm no baby," Leesa hissed, stomping her foot overhead.

"No offense, but you get my point." He finished lowering the backdrop to where it nearly touched the floor. "You'd better go. The orphans are lined up to sing."

"I bet if Lauren asked you, you'd jump at the chance," Leesa hissed. "You'll be sorry, you stuck-up snob."

At that, Lauren tiptoed up the rest of the flight of stairs to the tiny dressing room. She didn't dare get caught eavesdropping. She was embarrassed by Leesa's words, but in a funny way, they made her feel good too.

Flipping on the dressing room's overhead light, she quickly found the lavender makeup case, then turned to the row of costumes on hangers. Thumbing through the costumes, she found a marching band uniform, a drum majorette costume, three white coats for doctors, an Army jacket, a fire-fighter's coat and hat, and four gray rubber costumes with fins that looked like dolphins.

Lauren selected a white doctor coat, figuring it would substitute for a laundry man's white uniform. Picking up the makeup case, she then picked her way down the narrow wooden stairs to the stage below. She glanced overhead at the catwalk, but it was empty now. The stage was set with rows of cots, plus mops and buckets. All the orphans were in place to sing.

After handing Mrs. D. the make-up case and jacket, Lauren slipped into place to sing "Hard-Knock Life." The first time through, three gymnasts tripped over each other's feet to ruin the tumbling routine, but it went perfectly the second time through. Then Mrs. D. sat them down in a circle to review the next scene. Practicing on the stage was a lot different than practicing in the church basement, where they'd rehearsed till last Friday.

"It's coming together beautifully, kids," Mrs. D. said. "Now, for 'Tomorrow,' I want Jill center stage. The rest of you take seats in the first two rows. Don't be running up and down the aisles."

Grinning, Jill moved to the middle of the stage. She waited while footlights were adjusted to the exact color and brightness needed. Jill shaded her eyes against the glare and gave Lauren a tiny two-fingered wave. Lauren put two thumbs up in return.

When the music swelled for the introduction of "Tomorrow," Jill closed her eyes a moment, then opened them and stared toward the balcony as she sang. Lauren listened in amazement. How did that big clear voice come out of that shy little girl? As Jill flung her arms wide during the chorus, someone gasped. Then a collective shriek rose from the audience.

The upside down Christmas tree was dropping directly over Jill's head!

The screams startled Jill and she stumbled backward. The Christmas tree missed her head, but hit her foot. It crashed to the wooden stage, shattering its ornaments and silver lights. Tiny shards of glass spread across the stage. Jill dropped down and hugged her knees tight, her eyes squeezed shut.

Mrs. D. had been at the back of the theatre, listening. "Jill, are you all right?" she called as she jogged down the aisle to the stage.

Slowly Jill stood. "It was close, but I'm okay."

Lauren and Carl had both jumped from their seats at the crash. "How did that happen?" Carl asked. "Did the rope break?"

"I don't know." Lauren grasped the edge of the stage to climb up, but Mrs. D. held her arm. "Let me sweep up the broken glass first."

Lauren stood on tiptoes below the stage and stared where the tree had fallen. The rope was still attached to the trunk of the artificial tree. It must have snapped further up, or somehow come untied ...

Untied!

Lauren stared up toward the catwalk, but couldn't see it from below the stage. Was it empty now? It hadn't been empty just before rehearsal, she thought grimly. Leesa had been up there, supposedly to talk to Nick. Now Lauren had to wonder if that was her only reason for being on the catwalk by the ropes and pulleys. Has Leesa loosened the rope holding the tree? Leesa wouldn't mind at all if Jill was too hurt to perform.

Lauren tugged on Carl's shirt sleeve. "Just before rehearsal, Leesa was up on the catwalk bugging Nick to go out with her."

Carl's mouth fell open. "On a *date?*"

Lauren nodded. "He wouldn't, but that's not the point. Leesa was up there where all the ropes are tied that hold the backdrops and props up. She could have loosened the tree's rope while Nick was busy lowering that backdrop."

Grimly, Carl poked Lauren and pointed in Leesa's direction. She sat in the second row of seats, engrossed in her script as if nothing had happened. "She doesn't even seem surprised at the *accident*," he said.

Lauren studied Leesa, her eyes narrowed. "Wouldn't it be a tragedy if our star somehow couldn't perform? Leesa, no doubt, would step right into the lead."

"Lauren," Mrs. D. called. "Run downstairs and get me a broom and dustpan."

"Sure," Lauren said, hurrying down the winding stairs to the basement under the stage. At the foot of the stairs, a tiny bathroom was on the right. To her left was a workbench with an orderly arrangement of hammers, screwdrivers, and pliers. But where was a broom?

Lauren looked behind the broken pop machine called a "Cole Spa," which advertised ten-cent bottles of Coke. No brooms. No broom in the bathroom either. On the other side of the workbench was a huge metal fan attached to giant vents. Lauren figured this must be the swamp cooler she'd heard Todd tell Mrs. D. about. The theatre didn't have air conditioning, but this old swamp cooler blew cool air throughout the theatre in the summer.

On the other side of the swamp cooler was a light switch. Lauren flipped it on, and a dim bulb lit up a long narrow passageway. At the end of the hall, Lauren could see a furnace. A row of brooms, shovels, and plungers hung on a wall beside it.

Lauren hurried down the hallway, anxious to get what she came for and leave. She chose the wide push broom, since they'd have to sweep the whole stage floor. When she couldn't find a dustpan, she grabbed a blue plastic waste basket instead. Coming back down the passageway, Lauren brushed against a rough brick and snagged her sweater sleeve. A long piece of yarn now hung several inches down her wrist.

"Oh, man," she said, studying her unraveling sleeve. "Mom's going to kill me."

When Lauren came back upstairs, the stage manager and Nick were examining the tree. She crunched through glass fragments to hand the broom to Mrs. D. "What made it fall?" she asked Nick.

Mr. Blue stood the tree up. "That's the question of the hour, Missy." His words were clipped. "The rope isn't cut. Its knot somehow slipped loose."

"Ooo—ooohhhh—ooo," Carl intoned from below the stage. "It was our ghoulish little ghost, our scary little spook, our Phantom of the Opera House, our—"

"Enough, Carl," Mrs. D. said. "This isn't funny."

Tessa, one of the five-year-olds, began to whimper. "I want to go home," she said. "I don't want to be in this play."

"Me either," chimed in John, a first grader. He was short and fat, resembling a fire hydrant. His plump cheeks were reddened by wind burn. "My mom doesn't want me around crashing trees."

"There won't be any more crashing trees," Mrs. D. assured him. "Accidents happen."

Tessa wailed out loud then. "But Carl said it was a ghost! And I'm scared of ghosts!" She fell over in her seat and buried her face in her coat.

"Way to go, Carl," Leesa crowed.

"More like 'way to go, Leesa!'" Carl said. "Why were you up on the catwalk before rehearsal?"

Mrs. D. froze, hands gripping the broom handle. "You were up on the catwalk, Leesa? Why?"

Leesa turned several shades of purple and pink, but every time she opened her mouth, nothing came out. Lauren crossed her arms over her chest and waited. How would Leesa worm her way out of this mess? What could she say? That she'd been chasing a boy, trying to get him to take her out? How embarrassing to admit. For a brief second, Lauren felt sorry for Leesa.

For a very brief second.

Then Leesa said, "I think you're asking the wrong person, don't you?" She pointed a long, red fingernail at Nick. "*He's* the one who monkeys with the ropes. If anyone made the tree fall, he's your man."

"*Me?*" Nick said. He flushed a dark mottled red, and a tiny tic twitched at the edge of his right eyelid. "You're blaming *me* for this?" His voice was so filled with controlled anger that it was scarier to Lauren than yelling.

Mrs. D. swung around, dropping the broom with a sharp crack. "No one's blaming you, Nick. It was just an accident. No damage done—except maybe to this fake chandelier."

"You aren't letting him off that easy, are you?" Leesa demanded. "He could have killed somebody. It could be *me* next time!"

"We should be so lucky," Carl whispered to Lauren.

"She's just blaming Nick because he turned her down," Lauren muttered. "What a lowdown skunk she is."

"Okay, stop throwing wild accusations around," Mrs. D. said. "However, let me make one thing crystal clear." One by one, she looked at each child in turn. "That catwalk—and the dressing rooms, for that matter—are strictly off limits to anyone who doesn't have permission to be there. I don't want anyone falling off the catwalk or the dressing room stairs. It's a long way down to this hard stage floor."

"Mrs. D.! Mrs. D.!" Sadie Anne called from the wings. "Come here! There's a note from the ghost!"

Mrs. D. rolled her eyes at the stage manager. "What now?" she asked.

Lauren followed on Carl's heels as a dozen kids hurried up the steps to the stage. There in the wings, Mrs. D. was unpinning a paper from where it had been thumb tacked to the wall.

"What's it say?" Carl asked.

Sadie Anne's shining eyes were as big as silver dollars. "It said 'We don't want you here! Get the picture?'"

Mr. Blue glanced over Mrs. D.'s shoulder. "Maybe we should take the hint," he suggested.

Tessa broke out in fresh sobs. "I'm scared of ghosts. I want to go home."

"Come here, sweetheart," Mrs. D. said, holding out her arms. She cradled Tessa in her arms and stared hard at the note. She closed her eyes, then pressed a hand to her forehead as though checking to see if she'd contracted a sudden fever. "This is just a joke. You can sit on my lap for this next song. Then you'll feel better." Mrs. D. sat down at the edge of the stage.

Sniffling, Tessa crawled into the director's lap. John and Julia huddled around Mrs. D. While the stage manager swept the glass, Lauren fished her gray sweatshirt out of her backpack. Then, when Lauren raced back downstairs with the broom and waste basket, she slipped into the bathroom and changed. Now she looked like her plain old self, but she loved the comfort of it.

Down the narrow hallway, Lauren hung the broom back up on the wall by the furnace. Turning to leave, she spotted a small room behind the old heater.

Curious, Lauren peeked in, then felt for a light switch. She flipped it up, and a single overhead bulb blinked on. The weak light filtered down to reveal a huge movie poster glued to the back wall of the tiny room. Lauren stepped closer. The poster was taller than she was. It advertised *20,000 Leagues Under the Sea* with James Mason and Kirk Douglas.

Long cardboard tubes, at least fifty of them,

were stacked on a rickety table beside the poster. Lauren picked one up. Something was rolled up inside the tube. She pulled one out to discover another old movie poster. Carefully she re-rolled it and put it back.

Turning, Lauren bumped into something sharp. "Owww," she muttered, rubbing her leg where the corner of a wooden box had poked her. Turning out the light, she hurried back upstairs.

Mrs. D. was talking to Jill. "Could you try 'Tomorrow' again? Then, if there's time, we'll run through the scene where you hide in the laundry basket. Take it easy on your ankle and just stand *beside* the basket for now."

Jill craned her neck to look overhead, peering at the rafters. "Looks safe enough," she said. "I'm ready when you are."

Jill got through her solo this time without mishap, and after her final ringing note, everyone broke into wild applause. *Everyone except Leesa*, Lauren noted. She stood off to the side in the wings with her bottom lip sticking out.

"Am I on next?" Carl called, trying to glue on his little mustache with double-sided sticky tape.

"Here, it's crooked." Lauren peeled off the mustache, ignoring Carl's moans, then retaped it straight across his upper lip. "Why are you wearing this now?"

"It gets me into character." He twitched his upper lip. "This way I really *feel* the part."

"Then you'd better wear your uniform too, Mr. Bundles." Lauren held out the white jacket.

But when Carl slipped it on, the sleeves hung to his fingertips. Mrs. D. studied his coat, then

glanced down at the three little girls that had now crowded into her lap. "Lauren, can you do me another favor?"

"Find a smaller white jacket?" At Mrs. D.'s nod, Lauren peeled the oversized coat off Carl. He muttered his lines as Mr. Bundles while Jill hummed a few bars of "Little Girls." Lauren hurried up the steep staircase once again to the dressing room

Inside the dressing room, she hung up the first coat, then tried on the other two, since she and Carl were about the same size. She kept the smallest one. As she was shutting off the light, music for Jill's next song came through the speakers. Quietly, Lauren closed the door to the dressing room, then turned and looked below.

She hadn't realized it, but from the vantage point at the top of those stairs, she could see the whole stage, both up front and backstage. In the wings, Carl was heaping sheets and towels into a huge laundry tub on wheels, which would be used to hide Jill in later. Mrs. D. still sat near the front of the stage, with three small girls curled in her lap.

Fascinated by her view, Lauren paused on the top step. Clutching the coat and the banister, she peered down through the railings. The lady up in the lights room was adjusting the spotlight, focusing it into a tiny circle of bright light, then expanding it into a huge white circle covering most of the stage. Jill stood in the center, softly singing "Little Girls."

Lauren knew she ought to get downstairs with Carl's coat, but it was such fun to watch from up above. Slowly the spotlight grew smaller and brighter, leaving Jill standing in a white pool on the stage. Then it widened again. With the spotlight so bright, everything else faded into the shadows.

As Jill sang the last time through the chorus, Lauren's vision blurred and she blinked. She leaned closer, her stomach pressed against the railing. Were her eyes playing tricks on her? *What was that on the floor?*

While Jill sang, with clasped hands outstretched and face lifted, something long and black and thick inched its way across the floor, right into the circle of light surrounding Jill. It was heading straight for Jill's foot!

At that moment Lauren realized that she was the only one who could see the three-foot-long reptile slithering across the stage below. She did the only thing she knew to do, under the circumstances.

Lauren's horror exploded in a scream. "Snake!"

CHAPTER EIGHT

"Snakes Alive"

Lauren's scream was quickly drowned out by Jill's screech and the little girls' shrieks. The spotlight on Jill wobbled, moved in a tighter focus, then swung wildly upward to light up the red plush curtain overhead.

"House lights! House lights!" Mrs. D. yelled.

Lauren clutched the railing and froze. No way was she going down on that stage with a three-foot-long reptile loose! It seemed an eternity before the house lights came up. By that time, the stage had cleared. Not a single orphan was anywhere to be seen.

Oddly enough, however, the snake had stopped. It lay exactly where Lauren had spotted it, near the middle of the stage. Lauren frowned. Something looked fishy . . .

Grasping the railing, Lauren tossed the white jacket over her shoulder and tramped down the steps. When she reached the stage, she spotted something she hadn't seen from the top of the staircase: a long tan string.

And the thin string was attached to the head of a very long, very ugly, rubber snake.

Slowly, Lauren tiptoed out to center stage.

"No, Lauren, don't!" Mrs. D. called. "Let the stage manager get it."

"It's okay," Lauren assured her. "Unless this thing also has rubber fangs, it can't hurt me."

"Rubber fangs?" several orphans said in unison.

Lauren leaned down and, even though it was rubber, she lifted it by the string instead. "See? A fake."

Mrs. D. stormed up the steps to the stage then, stomped across to Lauren, and grabbed the rubber reptile. "*Who* did this? I demand to know right this minute!"

Someone in the wings giggled, but when the director swung in her direction, she stifled her laughter immediately. No one spoke up or admitted to being the culprit.

"Did you see who was pulling the string?" Mrs. D. asked. She was clearly angry, her arms folded, her lips a narrow red slash in her face.

Lauren shook her head. "The person must have been right under the stairs where I was sitting, though. The snake was being pulled in this direction. It would have gone right over Jill's foot."

As if in unison, several heads turned toward Leesa, who emerged from the wings. "What's everybody looking at me for?" she demanded.

No one answered, but Lauren bet they were all thinking exactly the same thing. *How badly did Leesa want the lead in the musical? Enough to drive Jill into quitting so Leesa could take over?* Lauren wouldn't put it past her.

Hands jammed in his back pockets, Nick slowly approached Leesa. "Where were you a few minutes ago?"

"What business is it of yours?" she snapped.

"I didn't appreciate being blamed for that tree almost hitting Jill, since you were up on the catwalk earlier too. So . . . I ask again. Where were you when the snake wiggled across the stage?"

Hands on hips, Leesa glared from Nick to Mrs. D. to Lauren to the little girls, and back to Nick again. "Well, if you *must* know, I was down in the rest room. I didn't know anything was going on till I heard some *idiot* scream." She stared directly at Lauren, in case anyone doubted who she referred to.

Mrs. D. sighed. "I don't think we're getting anywhere, but I do want to say one thing. I am *not* happy with these incidents. They're very disruptive to rehearsals. We seem to have a traitor in our midst—but who?" She turned in a slow, careful circle. "Frankly, I'm about ready to scrap the show entirely."

A dead silence fell over the whole group. Lauren saw Jill's shoulders slump, and she ached for her friend.

"Don't do that." Carl appeared from behind Mr. Bundles' laundry cart. His serious tone of voice contrasted with his crooked mustache. "Please don't quit. I have to confess. That's my snake."

"Carl! You?" Mrs. D. shook her head. "I can't believe you'd do these things. You know how precious the rehearsal time is."

Lauren stared. She couldn't believe it either. She had to press her lips together to keep from laughing out loud.

"Wait! Wait!" Carl protested, peeling off his mustache and sticking it in his pocket. "I only brought the snake, you know, for some laughs. Everybody's been so serious, what with Sadie Anne getting eaten by the cot, and Jill spraining her ankle. The rubber snake was supposed to remind us to have a good time." He took the rubber snake from the director. "This is my favorite pet," he explained to the group. "I haven't been allowed to have real pets ever since Mom found my newt dried up like a stick in my dirty gym socks." When no one laughed, he added, "That was a joke."

Carl shuffled his feet, but no one else moved. Lauren didn't dare say anything as her twitching lips would give her feelings away. She knew Carl didn't mean any harm—he just liked to clown around. Sometimes he got in trouble for it at school, but it had always been harmless fun.

Mrs. D. moved her mouth from side to side, chewing on the inside of one cheek, then the other. "Are you saying you had nothing to do with the lights going out that first night, or the tree falling, or the other accidents?"

"Absolutely 100 percent *nothing* to do with it."

Mrs. D. sighed and draped an arm over Carl's shoulders. "I believe you. I'm just glad you didn't give our star a heart attack with the snake."

Carl grinned at Jill. "Me too."

"However," the director said, "I now have four little girls who say they're quitting." She gestured in the direction of the long beige curtain at the side. It rippled, and several pairs of tiny tennis shoes peeked out from underneath. Tessa and Julia peered around the edge of the curtain. Julia's hair hung in pigtails; Tessa had one hunk of hair in a rubber band so that it stuck straight up like a little hair spout.

Carl looked at the little girls and grinned, but neither one moved. Neither one smiled back. Carl glanced at Lauren, who could only shrug. She didn't have a clue what he should do.

Finally, holding onto the string, Carl slowly swung the rubber snake around and around his head, then caught it. Sitting down cross-legged on the stage floor, he wiggled his finger at the little girls hiding behind the curtain. "Come here. It's just rubber." He thumped the snake on the floor hard enough to make it bounce.

Tessa and Julia giggled.

Then Carl wrapped the snake around his neck and tried to tie it in a knot. That didn't work, but he was rewarded with more giggles. Two more little girls peeked around the curtain.

Grinning, Carl stuffed the entire reptile down the front of his white jacket, receiving squeals of horror from the little girls. Then he pulled the snake's head out of his shirt collar, gazed lovingly into its face, then smooched it on its snake lips.

"*Ooooh! Yuk*," the little girls screeched. But they slowly emerged from behind the beige curtain, sidling up to where Carl sat in the middle of the stage.

"See?" Carl asked. "He won't hurt you." He turned the snake's face toward the girls. "Meet Max. He wants to give you all a big, big smacker."

"No!" they all yelled in unison. Three of them inched closer and closer, giggling the whole time. However, Tessa clamped her lips together in a ferocious scowl.

Carl then put Max's rubber nose against his ear

and pretended to be listening. "Max says he's going to cry if you girls quit the play. He slithered all the way to the theatre today just because he wanted to hear you sing."

"He did not," Tessa said, hands on hips.

"Yes, he did." Carl crawled to the side of the stage and lay down, propping himself on one elbow. Max, the rubber snake, still poked its head out of his shirt. "We're going to relax right here while you sing."

Mrs. D. covered her mouth, but Lauren could tell from her shaking hand that she was laughing. "Well, shall we take our places . . . and sing for Max?"

Without another word about quitting, they all found their places in the Orphan Chorus. Mrs. D. pushed the button on the CD player, and the introduction began. With no further incidents, the rehearsal continued through two more songs and a gymnastic routine.

At the end of the last song, Lauren ran downstairs to the rest room to get a drink of water. All that singing had dried out her throat, which already felt scratchy. She hoped she wasn't coming down with a cold. Too bad that old pop machine didn't work anymore, she thought.

Coming out of the bathroom, she paused and studied the small room. The workbench along one wall held jars of screws and nails of all sizes. Hanging right above were neat rows of various sized screwdrivers, hammers, wrenches and pliers. Among the nails were small old tin cans of Band-Aids and chewing tobacco. Lauren opened the Band-Aid box, but it was empty. The tobacco can held a large wadded up piece of aluminum foil.

Puzzled, Lauren dropped the foil in the palm of her hand and was surprised how hard it felt. Squeezing, she felt something inside. Slowly she unwrapped the foil. Inside was a necklace on a thin chain.

It was a silver heart with a clasp, and it looked vaguely familiar. Lauren pried the clasp open. Inside were two miniature pictures: a man and a woman. They seemed oddly familiar too. It wasn't until she heard Leesa's nasal voice whining about her "Sandy Song" at the top of the stairs that it dawned on Lauren where she'd seen the necklace. It was the one Leesa always wore.

Lauren stared at the pictures. Of course. They were Leesa's parents, only younger. How strange. What was Leesa's necklace doing in a tobacco can? And why would anyone their age wear a locket with her parents' pictures in it? They weren't dead or anything. They all lived on Elm Street.

Turning off the lights behind her, Lauren raced upstairs to catch Leesa. But the stage area was already empty except for the co-producers meeting with the stage manager.

"Bye, Lauren," they called as she grabbed her coat, then headed up the aisle to the lobby. Outside, she spotted Carl more than a block away, surrounded by four or five little girls. Lauren grinned. Looked like Carl and Max had a fan club. Leesa, however, was nowhere in sight. She must have left out the side EXIT door, Lauren thought, and gone home by way of the alley.

Dropping the necklace in her pocket, Lauren hopped on her bike parked in front of the barber shop and headed east. She'd call Leesa about the necklace when she got home.

She forgot about it, though, because her mom needed help when she got home making kringla and more rosettes for a Christmas Tea. A pile of braided heart-shaped paper baskets, traditional in Scandinavian homes for Christmas tree decorations, were on the dining room table. Lauren knew that these paper hearts would be filled with candy, cookies, and pieces of mistletoe.

"The chilled kringla dough is ready to roll out and bake," Lauren's mom told her when she walked into the kitchen. "If you do that, I'll make the rosettes. I got two new rosette irons today." She nodded at the long-handled snowflake-shaped irons on the counter.

"They look like branding irons," Lauren said. "Maybe we could brand Shawn with a rosette."

"Now, now." Beth Burk laughed and shook her head. "I've got the Crisco melted there and getting hot. The batter's done too." She put the rosette irons into the hot fat to heat.

Lauren got the chilled dough from the refrigerator, then floured the special kringla board. She dropped a teaspoonful of dough on it.

"How's Tillie today?" her mom asked, taking one of the hot rosette irons and dipping it in the batter. She returned the iron to the hot fat, immersing it and counting to twenty before lifting it out. The rosette was fried a golden brown.

"Well, she's really in the Christmas spirit," Lauren said, rolling the teaspoons of dough into ropes about six inches long. Then she made each rope into a circle and laid them on greased cookie sheets, making figure 8's with each one. "She donated money to some kid collecting for turkeys for the Food Pantry."

Beth Burk shook the rosette off the iron and dipped the iron again in batter. "Really? That's strange. The Food Pantry isn't giving out turkeys this year."

Lauren slid a full cookie sheet into the oven and set the timer for five minutes. It *was* strange, but not half as strange as the stuff happening during rehearsals. As they finished frying rosettes and baking kringla, Lauren told her mom all about Max and the crashing Christmas tree.

For the next hour Lauren ate all the kringla that broke or were misshapen, so by the time the baking was finished, she couldn't eat supper. "I think I'll do my homework and go to bed early," she told her parents. Shawn was out with his friends, the house smelled like warm cookies, and Lauren suddenly felt tired enough to sleep a week.

She was changing into her pajamas later and folding her jeans when Leesa's necklace fell out of her pocket. "Oh, shoot, I forgot." Holding the locket by its delicate chain, Lauren padded across the upstairs hallway to her parents' bedroom. She quickly found Leesa's number in the phone book and dialed it.

After five rings Lauren was ready to hang up when Leesa answered.

"Hi, Leesa, it's Lauren." A shout in the background was the only response Lauren received. "Leesa? Are you there?"

"What do you want?" Leesa snapped. "Make it quick."

Lauren's eyes narrowed. Here she was, trying to do something nice for this snob, and this was how she talked to her! She had half a mind to just hang up on her. She took a deep breath and let it out slowly.

"I've got something that belongs to you, a locket that—"

"My necklace!" Leesa said. "How'd you get it?"

"I found it in the basement at the theatre."

Leesa paused. "Oh, man, I took it off in the bathroom when I was combing my hair. The chain kept getting caught in my comb."

"I didn't find it in the bathroom," Lauren said. "It was wrapped in foil and hidden in a can."

"In a can?" Leesa demanded. "Who would hide my necklace in a can?"

"I don't know."

Leesa clicked her tongue against her teeth. "I bet I know. Jill found it in the bathroom and decided to keep it, didn't she? She *knew* it was my lucky locket. You're covering for your sneaky little friend. I should have known. Wait till I tell Mrs. D. what her little *star's* been doing!"

"You're wrong," Lauren said through clenched teeth. "Jill had nothing to do with it."

"Well, *somebody* stole it and hid it. You said so yourself." Another shout was followed by a slammed door.

"What's going on over there?" Lauren asked. "Who's yelling?"

"You dork, that's just the TV." She erupted with a phony-sounding laugh.

"Oh. Well, I'll bring the necklace to school tomorrow."

"See that you do," Leesa snapped, then hung up with a bang.

Lauren stared at the receiver in her hand, shook her head, and hung up. Trust Leesa to not even say thanks. What was wrong with showing a little gratitude anyway?

Lauren paused with her hand on the phone as a sickening thought struck her. Why had Leesa blamed Jill? Had Leesa hidden her own locket, intending to "find" it the next day and blame the theft on Jill? Or maybe she'd planned to slip the necklace in Jill's coat pocket, then "discover" it there later. Lauren wouldn't put it past her.

If Leesa was behind the tree falling and the rope left lying around, then planting stolen property on Jill might have been the next step in her plan.

Lauren padded back to her room to finish her math homework, and she laid the necklace beside the clothes she'd wear the next day. She peeked inside the locket again and stared at the two smiling faces. She had an uncomfortable feeling that while she'd been on the phone, those faces *hadn't* been smiling. Lauren knew that the yelling she'd heard was no TV, but two very real, very angry voices. Was that what Leesa lived with at home?

Lauren recalled Monday morning in the principal's office when she'd reported her money stolen, and Leesa had been tardy again. Something about a family emergency. At the time Lauren suspected she'd been crying.

Crawling into bed twenty minutes later to study for her social studies quiz, Lauren said a thankful prayer for her own parents. For the first time, she didn't envy Leesa Lyons one bit.

On the other hand she didn't feel very sorry for her either. Anyone who would hide her own necklace, then accuse Jill of stealing it just to get rid of her, was pretty low down.

About as slimy and low down, Lauren thought, *as Max, the rubber reptile.*

Tuesday's after school rehearsal had no surprises or disasters, and Mrs. D. applauded the cast and crew when they finished for the night. "Great job, kids," she said. "Let's do even better tomorrow night." She turned to Jill. "You're doing a fabulous job, Honey. You'll shine this weekend."

"Thanks." Jill ducked her head, but Lauren could see how pleased she was. After watching her shy friend be overlooked at school when choosing teams in gym, and left out of party invitations, and chosen last for group projects, Lauren was especially glad that Jill had the lead in the musical.

Leesa looks less than thrilled, Lauren thought as she observed Leesa's foul expression. Obviously Leesa still believed she was the best choice to star as Annie.

Mrs. D. had never announced it, but she must have told Leesa privately that she wasn't doing her dumb dog dance routine either. At any rate, Lauren had seen no such performance listed in the sample program the co-producers had brought to rehearsal.

Wednesday's rehearsal included the adult actors, so it was at 6:30 instead of right after school. Arriving at the dark theatre lobby that night, Lauren felt a thrill of excitement that Opening Night was just two nights away.

It was the day before Thanksgiving and the

store fronts and light poles were decorated with evergreen Christmas roping, lights, and giant ornaments. The twenty-foot-high Christmas tree already stood in the middle of the intersection of Broad and Pennsylvania Avenue. Decorated with strings of colored bulbs, it waited for Friday night's Tree Lighting, scheduled just before the Opening Night performance. They'd had snow flurries twice, but Lauren couldn't wait for the first real snowfall to blanket the town's Christmas tree. After the Tree Lighting, *Annie, jr.* would pull chilled carolers off the street and into the warm theatre.

Inside, as Lauren strolled down the theatre aisle, she could see Nick, Carl, and Mr. Blue wrestling with a newly painted street scene that they were lifting into place. Mrs. D. instructed the Orphan Chorus to sit in the two front rows to run through songs until the crew was finished onstage.

Lauren dropped her bag and winter coat on an empty seat, then hurried down front to join them. With music blaring, they went straight through "Maybe" and "Hard-Knock Life." When they finished, the stage set was ready and the crew gone.

Mrs. D. glanced up and grinned. "Good. Daddy Warbucks is here." She waved to the elementary principal who'd just arrived. "Let's hear the duet 'I Don't Need' with Annie and Daddy Warbucks next." She clicked through the CD music till she found the accompaniment. Jill smiled at the principal and followed him up on the stage.

During the duet, Lauren went to get a Kleenex out of her coat pocket and was surprised to see a folded piece of notebook paper lying on her coat. She opened it and read: "Come to the poster room when you get done."

Lauren glanced up, where Jill and the principal moved about the stage and sang. Lauren knew she wouldn't be needed again for a while. She'd told Carl about the poster room the day before. Surely there was no harm in showing him the posters really quick. Lauren slipped behind the crowd of chorus members and tiptoed down the steps to the basement.

The small room with the old pop machine was empty, but a light had been switched on beyond the swamp cooler, down the brick passageway to the furnace room. The poster room was right next to the heater. Overhead, music rose to a crescendo, then thumping noises indicated Jill cartwheeling across the stage and back.

Lauren scooted around the swamp cooler and down the narrow hallway. The bare bulb overhead lit her way, but the shadows it cast gave her the creeps.

In the furnace room, Lauren glanced first to the left and shivered at the long tunnel that burrowed under the theatre. Only three feet high, the walls and floor of the tunnel were dirt and broken bricks. Shuddering, she wondered if Todd ever had to crawl around under there. Looked like a great hiding place for spiders.

Turning toward the poster room, Lauren saw the light there was already on. "Aren't these great old posters?" she asked Carl. "My favorite—" Lauren stopped. No one was in the poster room.

A dusty baby buggy, two old fishing poles, and old Christmas decorations were stacked high on a battered desk. Another table held the dozens of cardboard tubes containing rolled-up movie posters. Back in the shadows, a huge octopus and submarine illustrated *20,000 Leagues Under the Sea*.

But there was no sign of Carl. Lauren braced herself. No doubt Carl was hiding, ready to jump out and scare her to death.

Lauren tiptoed into the room, quickly peeking behind the door and the cardboard boxes stacked high along one side. No one was there. She picked up a cardboard tube, tapping it thoughtfully against the table. The light was on, so Carl had obviously been there. But where had he gone?

From overhead, music swelled and Lauren knew their duet was nearly over. She had to get back upstairs. She returned the tube to the top of the stack, turned, and reached for the light switch. A second later the overhead light bulb blinked off.

At that exact same instant, the door to the poster room slammed shut. Lauren heard the dead bolt on the outside of the door slide smoothly into place.

CHAPTER NINE

"Trapped!"

Lauren froze for a moment, too stunned to move. The poster room was in total blackness, except for the thin strip of faint light under the door. She knew she was alone, but the sense of some other presence was so vivid that she felt the hair stand on her arms.

Lauren groped for the light switch and flipped it back on. That pushed the shadows back a bit, but with the door closed, the weak light cast an eerie glow on the waving octopus.

Overhead, Jill and the principal belted out the peppy song "Tomorrow." Lauren yanked and pulled on the door handle, then shoved and rammed her shoulder against the door, but it didn't budge. Heart pounding, and with sweat now running down between her shoulder blades, Lauren bit her tongue to keep from screaming.

Until the song ended upstairs, she knew no one would even hear her.

Fighting tears and trying to breathe around the pain in her chest, Lauren waited. Finally the song ended, and she wasted no time screaming while she kicked at the heavy wooden door. "Help! Somebody, help me down here! Help me!" she shouted.

Gasping for breath, Lauren listened as feet pounded overhead. Were the gymnasts practicing their dance number, or had they heard her shouts and were running for the basement stairs to rescue her?

"Oh, please find me," she whispered. A hard lump nearly closed off her throat.

Gazing into the dark corners, the poster room under the old theatre suddenly wasn't so fascinating. Just *threatening*. A great place for mice, in fact. Or rats. Lauren glanced overhead at the rough open-beamed ceiling. Or bats.

Pressing her ear against the door, Lauren's pulse quickened when she definitely heard footsteps clattering down to the basement stairs. "Help! Help me!" she screamed, willing her voice to carry down that hallway and past the swamp cooler.

But the footsteps stopped, and Lauren heard a door bang closed. "Shoot," she whispered. Someone was just using the bathroom. Well, she'd wait till they finished, then she'd scream again. If only there wasn't so much space between the poster room and the stairs, with that long spooky hallway, the huge furnace, and swamp cooler in between.

Breath coming in painful gasps, Lauren continued to pound and kick the door, praying that Carl or Mrs. D. would hear her. When she guessed that enough time had passed for that person to be done in the bathroom, she started yelling again. Until she brushed back her hair and felt her cheeks were wet, Lauren hadn't realized she was crying.

Just *wait* till she escaped from that room. She'd

kill whoever had locked her in there. Was it Leesa? Or was this another one of Carl's jokes? If it was, she'd strangle him with his own rubber snake.

Suddenly the music from "Easy Street" blasted out of the speakers up on stage. The adult playing Miss Hannigan must have arrived to practice her number with Rooster and Lily. Lauren continued to scream, but realized that no one in the bathroom would hear her over the music and dancing. Slowly Lauren slid down to the floor, her back against the door, so disappointed she felt ill. Sobbing, she listened to three pairs of feet tap dance on the stage directly over her head.

At the end of "Easy Street" Lauren pounded again on the door, with hands now scraped raw and bleeding. Her big toe felt broken too, from kicking the door so hard. She tried to bend her swollen toe, but couldn't. *Why* didn't someone notice she was missing? Why wasn't someone hunting for her?

When the introduction to "Easy Street" was played again, Lauren wiped her eyes and dabbed at her bleeding hands with a crumpled Kleenex. Gazing around the tiny windowless room, its walls painted black, Lauren searched for a weapon strong enough to break down the door. There was nothing.

Staring numbly, Lauren realized there was something odd about the *20,000 Leagues* poster glued to the opposite wall. From where she was slumped on the floor, she could see a sliver of yellow paint along the bottom edge of the poster.

She squinted, blinked, and stared. Or was it paint? Something about it didn't look quite right ...

Wait. That wasn't paint. Lauren scrambled on all fours across the tiny room, wincing at the pain as her bleeding hands touched the cement floor. That wasn't a strip of yellow paint under the poster. That was *light!*

Lauren ran her fingers along the jagged bottom of the poster. Sure enough, she could push her finger part-way underneath. That huge poster wasn't glued to the wall! It was glued to another door!

Breathing hard, Lauren brushed her hands up and down the poster, feeling for a door knob or handle or some way to open the door. At first she felt nothing, but the second time over, she found it: a tiny metal hook imbedded in the door. It was barely big enough to grab hold of. Lauren tried and tried, gripping the tiny hook with her fingers, then pulling. But her fingers slipped off, and the door stayed stuck shut.

Frantic, Lauren scanned the junk piled on boxes and the old desk. Her eyes slid past, then returned to the fishing poles. Could she somehow use one of those?

She grabbed one and tugged the heavy nylon fishing line loose from the reel. She slipped the fishing line through the hook in the door, then fed it through again to double its strength. Then she wrapped two feet of the fishing line around and around her wrist. Bracing her foot against the wall, she yanked the nylon line. It cut into her wrist, but she ignored the stinging pain and yanked again. Did the door budge? Disregarding the tears that sprang to her eyes, Lauren jerked hard one more time.

The door popped open an inch, moving the whole poster.

After unwrapping the nylon line from around

her wrist, Lauren grabbed the edge of the open door and pulled with all her strength. The door creaked as it swung inward, and Lauren found herself peering down another dark hallway. No light bulb lit this shorter hallway, but light filtered in where the hallway turned.

Lauren had no idea where it led, but she had to get out of that poster room. Hesitating only a moment, she headed down the hall, toward the dim light at the end. She hoped and prayed that this would lead her to safety.

Trailing her right hand along the cement wall, Lauren suddenly touched cold metal. Jerking back, she stifled a scream.

Squinting, she stared at what she'd touched. The whole right side of this odd hallway was lined with vertical water pipes, spaced apart like jail bars. Each pipe had spigots sticking out, aimed at cold steel plates behind them. The water spigots were dry. Puzzled at the strange contraption, Lauren wondered if this were the source of cold air used by the theatre's swamp cooler in the summer.

Hurrying down the hallway, Lauren turned a corner and almost bumped into the old pop machine. She'd come full circle! Lauren nearly cried, she was so relieved. No one else was in the basement room, and she could tell from the loud music and stomping feet that "Easy Street" was almost done.

Hands stinging, Lauren avoided the railing as she climbed the basement stairs up to the stage level. There, she shivered as a draft of frigid November air blew in from the EXIT door left ajar. She reached out to close it as the music stopped, but when she touched the handle, a voice on the other side of the door made her freeze.

Lauren blinked in surprise as she realized the voice was Elayna's " . . . I miss you too, Honey. It feels strange being apart for Thanksgiving tomorrow." She paused. "Yes, I'll spend the day with Mother. What? No, just the usual. Cranky as ever." She chuckled. "What? Oh, I'm sorry. I'm behind a building. The poor reception makes my cell phone cut out."

Elayna must be talking to her husband in New York, Lauren thought. She turned to back away, but Elayna's words stopped her cold.

" . . . you wouldn't believe the jinx on this poor play. Rumor has it that a phantom lives in this old opera house." She paused. "You're so right. It's a perfect setup for a mystery. I hardly have to invent a thing." She laughed at something, then added, "I couldn't have planned it better if I were the phantom himself." Lauren leaned close to the door and listened hard. "I'll wind things up tonight. The theatre owner loaned me a key, and I'll come back when it's empty to finish my research."

Lauren's hands were ice cold, either from the metal door handle, or the chill that ran down her spine at Elayna's words. It was true. Elayna *could* gain a lot from the weird happenings at the theatre. Rumors of it being haunted by a phantom would be great publicity when the book came out. Lauren scolded herself for even thinking such a thing, but it nibbled at the back of her mind as she hurried to take a front row seat.

Just then Mrs. D. turned and spotted Lauren. "Well, where were you all this time?" she asked.

"Are you okay?"

Lauren pushed her hands into the front pocket of her hooded sweatshirt. "Um, no, actually. I felt sick to my stomach. I was down in the bathroom."

"Oh, dear, I'm sorry." Mrs. D. knelt at the edge of the stage. "Anything I can do for you?"

"No, I think I'll just go home now."

She might as well. With Thanksgiving the next day, Lauren had a ton of cranberry salad to fix for her mom, then she'd help with several turkey dinners and the two dozen pies Carousel Catering had promised for the holiday. For caterers, holidays were big business. Lauren had practiced making the perfect pie crust for two weeks just for this job.

Lauren crumpled the note in her pocket, the one that had lured her down to the poster room. Carl was nowhere to be seen, but when he showed up to help cook the next morning, he had a *lot* of explaining to do.

But the next morning Carl was clueless. "Geez, Lauren, that's not even my handwriting," he said, smoothing out the crumpled note. "Couldn't you tell?"

"It's scribbly and messy, and you write scribbly and messy. Anyway, who else knew you wanted to see the poster room? In fact, who else even knew about it?" She pointed an accusing finger. "I only told *you*." Lauren brushed flour from her apron, sending up a billowing white cloud. "After your rubber Max prank, nothing would surprise me."

"Honest, Lauren, I never wrote the note, and I never locked you in there."

"If you tell me it was the Phantom of the Opera

House again . . ." Lauren frowned then as she recalled the overheard conversation outside the stage door.

"What?" Carl asked.

"Hmm?"

"Your face. You remembered something. Give."

"It's nothing. Really." Lauren couldn't bring herself to repeat Elayna's conversation. It made her friend sound so guilty! Lauren just couldn't believe Elayna was responsible for anything.

Just then Beth Burk came into the kitchen, stacks of Styrofoam pie carriers in her arms. "How's the crust coming?" she asked, rolling her eyes at Carl's speckled appearance. "Let's get at least half the flour into the crust, okay?"

Carl brushed at his purple T-shirt, which showed a dazed man in a crumpled parachute. Underneath, it said, *If at first you don't succeed, skip skydiving*. "If there's leftover crust, can I bake a pie to take home?" Carl asked. "My mom doesn't cook. Our turkey comes sliced in a box like a TV dinner. A real pie would save the meal."

"No problem. Although by the time we bake twenty-five pies, you may be out of the mood for one!"

Four hours later, Lauren fully agreed with her mom. She hadn't tasted any yet, but she didn't care if she ever saw another pumpkin pie. Sweaty from standing by the hot oven, Lauren longed to get outside to enjoy the unseasonably warm weather. "A bit of Indian summer," Lauren's dad said as he carried the last box of fresh pies out to the catering van.

When Lauren's parents drove off at noon loaded down with pies, cranberry salad, four complete turkey dinners, and homemade crescent rolls, she and Carl collapsed on the living room couch. Lauren leaned her head back and gratefully closed her eyes. Neither one said anything for a full five minutes.

"Doesn't feel much like Thanksgiving," Lauren muttered, "but at least we don't have to cater today."

Carl nodded. "For once, I'm glad I'm too young to drive." Neither of them was needed to make deliveries. "We worked four hours this morning. That's good money."

"True." Lauren kicked off her shoes and wiggled her cramped feet. Her black and blue big toe still ached from kicking the poster room door. "If my fifty dollars hadn't been stolen on Monday, I'd have earned enough today to pick up that Blue Willow platter. I just hope it's still there when I have enough money."

"So much for resting today, like Mrs. D. told us to." He flopped over sideways on the couch, snoring like a hibernating bear. "Can you believe tomorrow's Opening Night?"

"My folks want front row seats." Lauren wrinkled her nose. Her smelly feet competed with the pumpkin pie aroma, and her feet were winning. "I just hope Jill can do the play."

"I noticed her ankle was taped again yesterday."

"Yeah, it swells every time she dances on it." Lauren peeled off her socks to study her purplish toe. Her mom thought the nail would fall off. "I heard Leesa tell Mrs. D. yesterday that she could substitute for Jill if Jill couldn't perform. Leesa's memorized all of Annie's lines. She's even practiced the dance steps with a private dance instructor."

"Talk about sounding fishy!"

"No joke. She'd be thrilled if Jill had to quit."

At twelve-thirty Lauren dragged herself back out to the kitchen in search of food. She popped a Tupperware container of leftover stuffing in the microwave, then collapsed on a kitchen stool with a dish of cranberry sauce. "Help yourself," she told Carl, who already had his head in the refrigerator.

"No problem." He reappeared with a turkey leg and gnawed with energy. "Do you really think Leesa's behind the incidents at the theatre?" he asked, the turkey bone sticking out both sides of his mouth.

"Except the snake, you mean?" Lauren retrieved her stuffing when the microwave beeped. "I bet she threw the rope on the stage to trip Jill. She could have loosened the rope on the Christmas tree. As for the lights going out, she's danced in tons of recitals at that theatre. I bet she knows how the lights work as well as anybody."

"What about the spook stuff? The note pinned to the wall, locking you in the poster room . . . what's the point?"

"I've been thinking about that. *Maybe* if Mrs. D. had let her do that stupid dance with her stuffed dog, Leesa would have left the play alone. But maybe when she learned she was only an ordinary orphan like the rest of us—she just couldn't take it."

"She flipped out?" Carl drummed his greasy fingers up and down the counter as he hummed creepy organ music. "If she can't be a star, then she'll stop the play?"

"I could believe it. You know how mean she is."

Lauren finished off her cranberry sauce and set the dishes in the sink.

Carl waved the turkey leg in Lauren's face. "I bet she wrote that note, then hid behind the furnace. When you came down, she locked you in."

"Except how did she know I told you about the poster room?"

Carl tapped his turkey bone on his plate as if he were playing a drum. "I bet I know. I told Nick about it while we put that new scenery up. Leesa was hanging around bugging him. I bet she heard me."

"Makes sense." Lauren admitted privately that she liked the idea of Leesa being the culprit better than any other explanation that had reared its ugly head lately. It just couldn't be Elayna. A phantom maybe? Lauren couldn't swallow that either.

What could Leesa have up her sleeve next? she wondered ominously. Whatever it was, in order to ruin Opening Night, it would have to be something *big*.

CHAPTER TEN

"Nightmare Revisited"

After Carl left at one o'clock to go home to his own Thanksgiving dinner, Lauren wandered around the house, feeling lost. Her parents wouldn't be back from their out-of-town deliveries for several hours. Thankfully her brother was working. "I'd be stupid not to take holiday pay just to stay home with *you*," he'd told her that morning.

Lauren was glad he was gone, but a sudden wave of loneliness caused her to shiver. Being home alone on the holiday was hard. There was nothing on TV but football. She stuck a tape in the VCR and half-watched the library's *Annie* movie that her mom had checked out for her. Unfortunately, watching the heroine sing and dance on the TV screen doubled her worries about their own performance the next night.

As the last echoes of "Tomorrow" died away and the credits rolled, Lauren glanced at the clock: 3:30. Her parents were taking forever making deliveries. She hoped the van hadn't broken down in some little town where all the service stations were closed.

"I know." Lauren snapped her fingers. "I'll take

Tillie some flowers. Elayna's sure to be at the nursing home too."

Replacing her flour-covered T-shirt with a navy sweater, she grabbed her winter coat, jammed her knitted hat down over her ears, and cut a bouquet of bronze and gold chrysanthemums. Burying her nose in the flowers, she walked the three blustery blocks to Bethany Manor. Dried leaves skittered down the street in the same direction she walked, *scritch-scratching* along the pavement. Overhead, curled brown leaves still clung to the oak trees, but crunchy maple and elm leaves filled the gutters and covered most front yards.

Now that she had someone to share the holiday with, Lauren's spirits soared in spite of her tired back, scraped hands and swollen throbbing toe. Her spirits stayed high until she arrived at Tillie's room. It was wall-to-wall people: Tillie, Alma, Elayna, Ella, Tillie's son Don—and a policeman.

Lauren hesitated in the doorway, uncertain whether or not to go in. Just then Elayna turned and noticed her. "Lauren! Come in and join the party."

Feeling like an intruder, Lauren stepped into the room. The policeman turned and nodded. "Happy Thanksgiving, Lauren."

"You, too, Barry. What's going on?" Lauren looked for a vase for the mums, but couldn't find one. She held her bouquet awkwardly in front of her.

"I hate doing this on Thanksgiving," the young police officer said, "but apparently we've got a theft ring operating in the nursing home."

"I knew it," Alma snapped. "Would anyone listen

to me? Would you? I warned you."

"Mother, please, you're not helping." Elayna's words were slow and calm.

"But she's right." Tillie's voice quavered. "Alma warned me about giving money to people, but I only wanted others to have a nice holiday."

"Of course you did," Don said, kneeling beside Tillie's chair.

"What exactly happened?" Lauren asked.

Barry ran his hand through his hair and rubbed the back of his neck. "It's a nasty business. The staff called me when they realized that at least five residents had reported giving to someone collecting for charity."

"Is something wrong with that?" Lauren asked.

"No one is allowed in the nursing home asking for money. One person collected for United Way, another one for the Red Cross. Both these charities swear that no one from their organization was here. One person said he was collecting money for the Food Pantry."

"I remember Tillie talking about that. Some guy with a limp said they were giving away turkeys, right?" Lauren waved her bouquet back and forth. "I asked my mom—she works at the Food Pantry—but she said they weren't giving out turkeys this year."

"That's just the tip of the ice berg, I'm afraid," Elayna said. "Money is missing, and several people have reported rings and watches stolen."

"Like Leo's diamond ring," Tillie cried, lips quivering.

"Even worse," Alma snapped, "was that young soldier who visited, that nurse's brother. Ha!"

"You mean Jenny's brother?" Lauren was confused now. "What about him?"

"He was an impostor," Alma said, almost crowing. "I told you his shoes were very odd for a soldier."

"But Jenny's brother *was* here," Lauren protested to Barry. "I talked to his sister, who showed me his picture."

"This one?" Barry asked, holding out a small photograph.

Lauren glanced at it briefly. "Yes, that's him. Bobby, I think his name was." Elayna took Lauren's bouquet and stuck the mums in a plastic pitcher full of water.

"This *is* Bobby," Barry agreed. "But it's *not* the young solider who claimed to be Bobby and took donations from Tillie and a number of other residents."

"It's not?" Lauren held the picture out to Tillie. "Are you sure?" Suddenly very warm, she slipped off her coat and stuck her hat in the sleeve.

Tillie shook her head. "The soldier who was here had curly blond hair. Jenny's brother is practically bald."

"And the mustache," Alma piped up. "Jenny's brother doesn't have a mustache, but that phony who collected for the 'cold little orphans in Germany' did."

"I can't believe that someone would come into a nursing home—at the *holidays* yet—and steal from the elderly," Ella exclaimed. "What kind of person would do such a thing?"

"A con artist. A cunning person," Barry said. "Any punk can grab a gun and rob you, but it takes a smart person to be a con artist."

Don twisted his hat around and around by the brim. "But to commit crimes against the elderly—that takes a real low life."

"Cases are even worse against elderly people still living at home," Barry said, closing his notebook and sticking it in his shirt pocket. "Con artists know that older folks often keep money from real estate or insurance at home, and they tend not to be suspicious of strangers. They believe in people." He smiled at Tillie and then at Alma. "It's not true for you two ladies, but *some* older people are weak and frail too, which also invites crime."

Alma snorted. "I'd like to see some thief try to steal from me. I'd run him down with my wheelchair."

"They don't always hit you over the head to steal," Tillie said quietly. "My friend, Henry, lost money on a phony Lonely Hearts Correspondence Club after his wife died. Some lady wrote wonderful letters to him—she said she wanted to come here and marry him, but needed money to move from California where she lived. He sent her the money, but never heard from her again."

"That's terrible," Lauren burst out. "How could somebody do that?"

"That's not all," Alma said. "That ding bat across the hall who thinks she's Ginger Rogers got taken for a bundle."

"Who's Ginger Rogers?" Lauren asked.

Elayna and Ella laughed. "It's before your time, but she was a famous dancer," Elayna explained. "She danced with Fred Astaire, who's also before your time."

"I wasn't finished!" Alma snapped. "That lady paid half her savings for a lifetime membership in a dance studio." She cackled. "The old fool."

"I'm afraid that none of this surprises me," Barry admitted sadly. "About 60% of the fraud victims in this country are elderly."

"It happens to young people too," Tillie said. "Lauren had some money stolen last week."

"Yes, at school," Lauren said. "I haven't got it back either." She turned back to Barry. "What can you do to help Tillie?"

"First I need to interview the residents and see how widespread the thefts are. I also need complete descriptions of the people who did this." He put his cap back on and pulled it down low. "The staff asked me to talk to the residents tomorrow morning about what's happened so no one else falls victim to this swindling group."

When Barry left, Lauren glanced out the window and gasped. "What time is it?" she asked. "It's dark already."

"Gets darker earlier and earlier, especially without Daylight Savings Time." Don pushed up his long flannel shirt sleeve to see his watch. "It's only 5:20, but it might as well be midnight."

"I've got to go." Lauren grabbed her hat and coat. "Happy Thanksgiving, everybody."

"Wait, Lauren. I'll give you a ride." Elayna reached for her down-filled coat where it lay across the foot of Alma's bed. "I'm heading back to the motel myself."

"Why?" Alma demanded. "You just got here."

"Now, Mother, I've been here since ten this morning. We had a tasty dinner, and we enjoyed the music program in the chapel together." Elayna leaned down close to her mother. "I'll be back tomorrow, bright and early. Why don't you go to bed early tonight yourself?"

"Ha." Alma scowled. "Plenty of years to lie down in my coffin. Stop trying to push me into my grave before my time."

Elayna rolled her eyes at Lauren. "I want to go talk to the nurse about Mother's medication. It'll just take a minute, then we can go."

"We need to go too," Don said. He and Ella followed Elayna out the door, waving as they left.

Alma watched them leave, pursing her lips till they looked like twin prunes. "I don't need Laney to talk to my nurses behind my back. What secrets are they keeping from me?"

Lauren was shocked at the nasty tone of her voice. "I'm sure Elayna wouldn't have secrets from you," she protested.

Alma backed her wheelchair around to face Lauren. "You think she doesn't keep secrets?" She nodded grimly. "I'll tell you a secret. Without a bestseller this time, Laney's career is down the tubes." A look of satisfaction passed over her face, then disappeared.

Lauren collapsed on Tillie's bed. "What do you mean?"

Alma's nostrils flared. "I happen to know things. People treat me like I'm stupid, but I know things." She clamped her lips together.

Lauren hesitated. Elayna's career problems were none of her business. On the other hand, she cared about her friend.

Alma smacked her lips and sat up straighter.

"Laney's husband called her on her cell phone here last night, and I happened to overhear. I wasn't *trying* to overhear, you understand. It just couldn't be helped."

Tillie tugged on Lauren's arm. "That's not true. Elayna took her call out in the hallway, but Alma followed her and listened."

"Hush up, you blabbermouth." Alma scowled at Tillie, then turned back to Lauren. "I happen to know that her publisher went out of business two months ago. Some big corporate take-over. Her books are going out of print already. No books to sell means no money."

"Oh, no. That's terrible," Lauren said.

"Yes, terrible." Alma's eyes almost twinkled. "She's obsessed with this next book. She has to find another publisher. That's why she's so anxious to get back to the motel to pound on that portable computer of hers."

When Elayna returned a moment later, Lauren jumped up, ready to leave. Elayna kissed the top of her mother's curls, but Alma pushed her away. Shrugging, Elayna took Lauren by the arm and marched her out the door. They were halfway down to the finch cage before Elayna spoke.

"If I get as sour as my mother in my old age, I hope somebody stuffs a rag in my mouth."

Lauren giggled. "Alma *does* have a lot of spice, Henry says."

Elayna giggled. "Part garlic, and part hot chili powder!"

Coat collars pulled high, they pushed out into the cold night air. Shivering, Lauren scanned the parking lot. "Which way?"

"My rental's over there."

Head down, Lauren followed Elayna to the west end of the parking lot where a gray four-door with a rental sticker was parked. Elayna fished keys out of her pocket, unlocked Lauren's door, then her own. "I keep forgetting I'm just in Story City and don't need to lock my doors," she said, climbing in behind the wheel.

"I used to think that too, but now I'm not so sure," Lauren admitted. "I would never have guessed Bethany Manor would be invaded by thieves."

"That *was* a shock." Elayna switched on the headlights, then swung onto Lafayette Avenue. "Say, I got the key to the Carousel building from the lady at the Chamber of Commerce office. I planned to stop there tonight to take some notes and snapshots before going to the motel to work." She shifted in the seat and grinned at Lauren. "Want to come with me?" Her face was eerie in the greenish light from the dashboard.

"Sure. Could we drive by my house on the way? If my parents are home, I need to tell them where I'm going."

"No problem." They turned on Cedar, then north on Grand, but when they slowly passed Lauren's house, the catering van was nowhere to be seen. "Now what?" Elayna asked.

"Will you be at the Carousel long?"

"Just long enough to take some pictures and make a few notes. I want to use the Carousel in my next book, and I need some details."

"Sure I'll go," Lauren decided. "I've never been inside the building when the horses are in storage."

"Sounds kind of creepy, doesn't it?" Elayna asked, driving on down the dark street, then turning east on Broad. She pulled into the parking area at the top of the hill behind the empty swimming pool. Slamming the car doors, they walked down the sloping sidewalk to the Carousel.

Night lights dimly lit the inside of the building. Lauren pressed her face against the glass in the sliding doors while Elayna hunted for the keys in her purse. "Here they are." She unlocked the padlock on the door, then inserted a second smaller key into the security lock. The tiny light turned from red to green. Then with a hefty shove, Elayna slid one of the green doors open far enough for them to squeeze inside.

Lauren was immediately struck by two things: the frigid air and the spooky look of the Carousel without its horses. She knew that every year the carved, painted horses were stored for the winter in temperature-controlled boxes built especially for them, to keep them from drying and cracking in the subzero building during the winter.

"Even without the breeze, it must be twenty degrees colder in the building than outside," Elayna said, rubbing her hands together.

Lauren nodded, turning slowly in a circle, watching her breath appear in small, smoky puffs. For her, however, it was no longer 30 degrees in the Carousel building . . . Instead it was close to 100, and the month was May. She felt sweat break out under her coat while the hair bristled on the back of her neck. Being in the deserted building at night brought the whole terrifying scene back.

"What is it, Lauren?" Elayna asked. "You look

like you've seen a ghost."

"I guess I did." Lauren shivered and wrapped her arms tightly around herself. "Being here— especially at night—gives me the creeps."

"I'm sorry. I'd forgotten about your ordeal when I invited you along."

"No, that's okay." She walked around the out- side of the Carousel, touching the red and green tub that was usually whirling, but was now perfectly still. Lauren stopped beside Elayna and turned in a slow circle. "It isn't hard to remember crawling on my stomach in the dark, then getting grabbed when I tried to escape."

Elayna whipped open her notepad while Lauren talked. "How long were you trapped in here that night?" she asked.

"I don't know." Lauren turned from the Wurlitzer Military Band organ and pointed to the rack of shirts and bags for sale. "I was hiding in that skinny cupboard over there when he spotted me."

Elayna's eyes widened in horror. "You crawled into that tiny space?"

"It was the closest place I could find at the time. I thought I was dead meat."*

"I'm so sorry that happened to you," Elayna said. "We *both* kept our guardian angels busy that night!"

Lauren laughed, but had to agree. She hadn't expected to leave the Carousel building alive that night. Shaking off the memory, she turned to where Elayna was studying the framed photos along the walls. Each showed various stages of restoration of the 1913 Herschell-Spillman Carousel as the horses were repaired, rebuilt, and repainted. Fifteen minutes later, Elayna stuck her pencil behind her ear, snapped her notebook shut, and slipped it in her shoulder bag.

"I have what I need," she said. "Ready to go?"

"I'd better. I'm sure my parents are home by now."

And when they arrived five minutes later, the catering van was indeed in the driveway. The hood was up and her dad's tool box was in the driveway. Apparently engine trouble had delayed them. Lauren only hoped they'd made their deliveries on time first.

Lauren opened the car door and climbed out. "Good luck with your writing tonight," she said.

"Thanks. I can't wait to get to my computer. Get some rest now. Tomorrow's the big day." With a wave, Elayna backed out of the drive and turned north again.

Lauren stood in her dark front yard and watched the rental car's tail lights grow smaller and smaller. Elayna stopped at Broad at the stop sign, but Lauren frowned as the car turned west, heading uptown instead of east to the Viking Motor Inn, where Elayna was staying.

Hadn't Elayna said she was going right to the motel to work? Then why turn the opposite direction? Nothing uptown was open on Thanksgiving. Unless . . .

Unless Elayna was headed up to the theatre. From what Lauren had overheard the day before, Elayna had a key to the theatre too. Now that Lauren thought about it, though, it seemed strange. Would Todd really give a stranger a key to the theatre? Anyway, why did Elayna need to go there when it was empty?

Lauren crunched through dried leaves in the yard and went inside, an uneasy feeling stirring in her stomach. How much "research" did Elayna really need to do? And why hadn't she mentioned it just now to Lauren?

An ugly suspicion struggled to enter Lauren's thoughts, and she was only half successful in fighting it down.

*Carousel Mystery #1 *A Spin Out of Control*

CHAPTER ELEVEN

"Discovered"

Promptly at 9:00 the next morning, Lauren passed through the doors to the F & M Bank, her money clutched tightly in her hand. This time she hadn't let her twelve dollars out of her sight. After making her deposit, she checked the clock in the lobby: **9:04**.

She wasn't due at rehearsal till 9:30. Mrs. D. wanted a quick run-through of two Orphan Chorus songs, then two tumbling routines for the five gymnasts. Shivering on the sidewalk in front of the bank, Lauren studied the low-hanging slate-gray clouds and debated what to do. There wasn't enough time to go home and make it back by 9:30.

"I know what I'll do." She wrapped her scarf carefully around her face. She wanted to cut the wind without disturbing her new hairdo. She patted her smooth blonde hair where the tiny butterfly clips held it off her face. With her hair curled, she looked at least fourteen, Lauren thought. At least, she hoped Nick would think so.

In the meantime, she'd visit the antique store to check on that Blue Willow platter. In spite of the cold wind, Lauren felt warm inside as she pictured that platter on the dining table for every holiday: holding a roasted turkey, or Christmas cookies, or the coconut-covered Easter Bunny cake her mom made every year. But the best thing was imagining her mom's face when she unwrapped the platter on Christmas morning.

Pulling on her fuzzy green mittens, Lauren jogged down Pennsylvania Avenue's brick street. She turned at the alley behind the post office and half-ran to the Antique Alley store tucked in between the tea room and the Christmas Stocking store. Breathing hard, Lauren inhaled a mouthful of wet yarn fibers. Yanking her scarf off her face, she spit till she got rid of them.

When she pushed open the door to the antique store, a pewter chime in the shape of butterflies clinked musically, announcing her entrance. A woman in a pink sweater and glasses that hung on a chain around her neck glanced up from where she dusted a display of cut glass bowls and vases. The woman had painted-on eyebrows; they were different sizes and shapes every time Lauren saw her.

"Yes? Oh, hello, Lauren."

"Hi." Heart pounding, Lauren hurried to the small adjoining room to check on the platter. She knew exactly where it was from looking at it so often. It was in an out-of-the-way spot, sitting on a hand-crocheted doily. She turned the corner, but instead of the large oval blue and white platter, the space was occupied by a fluted red glass bowl full of wax fruit.

Lauren's heart stopped, then pounded wildly. It was gone! She scanned the back room quickly, in case it had been moved. It wasn't there. Tears welled up in her eyes, and she blinked hard. If only her money hadn't been stolen at school last week! She would have had enough to buy it then.

Shuffling back to the main room, Lauren waved half-heartedly to the sales woman on her way out the door. The woman stuffed her dust cloth into the pocket on her oversized apron. "Come to see your pretty dish?"

Lauren nodded glumly. "Who bought it?"

"A lady from Sioux City was passing through, and she *oohed* and *ahhed* over it. Her grandmother had had one just like it." She paused and smiled, wearing thin arched eyebrows today. "I told her it was already spoken for."

Lauren's heart quickened. "You did?"

The woman moved behind the glass counter where an antique cash register rested. Stooping, she reached underneath for a flat box and lifted it onto the counter. Inside the box, encased in a long sheet of bubble wrap, was Lauren's Blue Willow platter. "I saved it for you," she said.

"Oh, thank you. I almost have enough money. I just put more in the bank." Lauren took off her mittens and stroked the ceramic dish. Three blue Chinese figures still posed on the bridge, one carrying a fishing pole on his shoulder. "Should I pay you what I have now, and the rest later?"

"No, just pay me when you have it all."

"It'll be a week, maybe two at the most," Lauren said. On a back wall, an old cuckoo clock chirped while a red bird popped out a little door six times. "Mom has lots of catering jobs lined up now, mostly Christmas parties."

"Well, you bring the money in when you can."

"Okay." Knowing the cuckoo clock was wrong, Lauren stretched her neck and tried to read the woman's watch. "Can you tell me what time it is?" she finally asked.

"9:25." The woman re-wrapped the platter, slipped it in the box, and put it back below the counter.

"I've got to go. Rehearsal at the theatre in five minutes." Flinging her scarf over her shoulders, Lauren stepped around an old wooden sled and headed out the door. "Thanks again!"

When she arrived at the theatre, she noticed a difference right away. Electricity seemed to crackle in the air, and everyone chattered excitedly in little groups. Maybe it was the Opening Night jitters Mrs. D. had warned them about.

She scanned each group for Jill, wondering about the star's jitters. Lauren knew she herself would be paralyzed if she were the star. Lauren frowned when she couldn't find her. Usually Jill was early, studying her script while she waited for rehearsal to begin. She wasn't with Daddy Warbucks, or Mrs. D. either.

Maybe Jill was down in the public rest room, Lauren thought. She ran down the stairs to the ladies room, but it was empty. Back upstairs, Lauren strode down the aisle to the stage, peeling off her coat as she went. Onstage, the backdrop was already in place for the first scene. The brick building sported a big sign: "Hudson Street: Home for Girls." Perched on the edge of the stage were three orphans from the first song, already dressed in night shirts and pajamas.

"Have you seen Jill?" Lauren asked the third

grader who played Molly.

"Nope. Not yet," she said, watching her feet bounce as she kicked the edge of the stage.

Lauren could feel the panic rising in her even as she told herself to calm down. "Nothing's wrong," she muttered. And yet, she remembered the coiled rope, and the falling tree. Accidents? Maybe. Or attempts to remove Jill from her starring role?

Where *was* Jill?

Lauren checked the tiny bathroom downstairs under the stage. Empty. She bounded up the short flight of stairs, opened the EXIT door and peeked outside. No one there either. Up a few more steps to the stage, Lauren peered behind the backdrops and the beige curtains at the sides. No one.

Breathing hard, she tiptoed up the stairs to the Garbo dressing room. Although strictly forbidden up there, Lauren had to check it out. A vision of Jill lying unconscious spurred her on. What if Leesa had found Jill alone and made sure this time that she couldn't perform that night?

Flipping on the light in the tiny dressing room, Lauren checked behind the door. No one. Annie's red dress hung on the nearest hanger, and her red wig and makeup were on the table by the mirror.

Down the steps, Lauren slipped behind the backdrop and trotted as quietly as possible to the other side of the stage, then up to the King Kong dressing room. Also empty.

She peered behind that door too. It had been signed by "The Musical Vaughns, 1929," but no one was there now. *Now what?* Lauren thought as she descended from the second dressing room. A sense of urgency gnawed at the edges of her mind. At the foot of the stairs she glanced up to the catwalk, but it was empty too.

"What a great place for a spy," Lauren whispered, bending her neck backwards.

Biting her lip, an idea slowly took shape in her mind. Lauren studied the black-painted iron ladder rungs attached to the wall. They led right up to the catwalk. From up there, a person could see everything going on below—and *everybody*.

All week long, Lauren's fear had grown with each accident or unexplained happening. The fear growling in the pit of her stomach warned her that today—the day of the play—something really awful would happen to eliminate Jill as the star and make room for someone else.

Everything pointed to Leesa. This morning's dress rehearsal would be her last chance to get rid of Jill and take over the musical's leading part.

If only Carl or Nick were there, they could help her! But Lauren had heard Mrs. D. say they were back at the church, helping the co-producers load up boxes of printed programs and tickets. So much for impressing Nick with her new hairdo.

Glancing over her shoulder to make sure no one saw her, she gripped the bottom metal rung. Taking a deep breath, Lauren stared straight at the wall and climbed up toward the catwalk.

Halfway up, her stiff shoulders and fingers ached. Lauren looked sideways and down, and nearly lost her grip. The wood floor below her would break bones if she fell. Legs trembling, Lauren bit her lip and stared at the black wall in front of her face. *Don't look down!* she warned herself. Step by step, she climbed toward the catwalk.

Without warning, music for "Hard-Knock Life" blared from the loud speakers. Lauren jumped, her right foot slipped off the rung, and she banged her teeth against the metal bar in front of her face. Feet scrambling, she found the rung again. She could taste salty blood from where she'd bit her tongue.

Abruptly the music stopped. Mrs. D.'s voice echoed from below. "Gymnasts, up onstage. Do the routine with your props. Orphan Chorus, line up in the wings."

Lauren froze. If anyone peeked behind the backdrop, they'd see her. Lauren forced herself to climb the last three steps. At the top of the ladder, she crawled onto the catwalk's platform. On hands and knees, Lauren waited for the nausea to pass. Then she opened her eyes and looked twenty-five feet below.

Dizzy, she had a sudden vision of the catwalk coming loose and plunging to the stage below. Lauren shook her head and forced herself to keep looking.

The catwalk gave her a bird's-eye view of everything below, including the five gymnasts doing acrobatics while the chorus sang "Hard-Knock Life." The gymnasts danced with mops and buckets, swept with brooms, and pretended to wash windows in Miss Hannigan's orphanage. Everything looked exactly as it should.

Then Lauren caught a quick movement out of the corner of her eye.

Motionless, Lauren watched as Leesa stepped back from the last row of the chorus group onstage and slipped behind the beige curtain. She disappeared for a moment, then emerged by the stairs to the Garbo dressing room. Barely breathing, Lauren watched her sneak up the stairs with frequent glances over her shoulder.

Leesa disappeared into the dressing room, but left the light off. A full minute passed, then she reappeared at the dressing room door. Grasping the wooden railing, she slipped smoothly down the stairs again.

Lauren squinted. Something was odd about Leesa's appearance. She looked . . . lumpy. Sitting back on her heels, Lauren watched Leesa slip behind the beige curtain instead of rejoining the chorus onstage. What in the world was she doing? Was she going to the basement? Why had she looked so lumpy?

"I know why," Lauren suddenly whispered. And she had to stop her.

Crawling back to the catwalk's ladder, Lauren took a deep breath and placed one foot on the top rung. Then, not allowing herself to look down, she swung over and put her other foot on the ladder. Her fingers gripped the iron rung till her knuckles ached, but she started down.

Step by step, she moved in jerky rhythm with the chorus. No one, unless they happened to peer behind the backdrop, would see her clinging to the wall.

Finally at the bottom, Lauren stepped gratefully back on solid ground. Lauren was glad that "Hard-Knock Life" was such a boisterous song, with lots of tumbling and clanking from the mops and buckets. Stiffening her wobbly knees, she crept along behind the props and backdrops to the other side of the stage. Crouched low, she slipped behind the chorus to head down the stairs to the basement.

However, Lauren noticed that the door leading into the main theatre was ajar. Just to make sure, she peeked at the rows of empty seats and stared up at the balcony. No sign of Leesa. Lauren stood there trying to decide which direction to go.

Just then a cold draft of air made Lauren shiver, and she realized the side EXIT door was open about an inch. Tiptoeing over to the door, she found it propped open with a stick. That must be where Leesa went! The stick kept the door from shutting and locking her out.

Glancing over her shoulder, Lauren made sure no one onstage could see her. Then she pushed open the EXIT door and slipped outside, making sure the stick was still in place. Outside, the wind blew her hair in her eyes, blinding her for a minute. She brushed her hair back and held it.

At first she didn't see Leesa anywhere. She was almost ready to go back inside the warm theatre when a movement near the alley caught her eye. There, leaning over the green garbage dumpster, was Leesa. She lifted the big black plastic lid and tossed something inside.

Lauren jogged around red-twigged bushes and bare trees on dead grass that muffled her steps. "Fancy meeting you here," she said when she reached the dumpster.

Leesa jumped and whacked her hand against the lid. "What? How dare you sneak up on me?" She dropped the lid with a bang, but not before Lauren saw what she'd tossed there.

She grabbed Leesa's arm and pulled her aside.

Lifting the dumpster lid, Lauren pulled the red curly wig from where it lay among used cups and crumpled popcorn boxes. "And hand over Jill's costume. I see your lumpy body. Her red dress is stuffed up your shirt."

"I— I—" Leesa stammered, her face turning nearly as red as the wig. "It's not what you think."

"Oh sure." Lauren waved the wig in Leesa's face. "You're just keeping Jill's costume safe for Opening Night, right? You're hiding it so the Phantom of the Opera House can't take it and ruin Jill's performance, right?" Lauren's next words were like chunks of ice in the silence. "Your jealousy has gone too far. I'm telling Mrs. D."

"No, wait." Leesa grasped Lauren's arm, but Lauren shook her free and turned to leave. "Please wait!"

Lauren halted at the pleading panic in Leesa's voice. She watched Leesa reach under her sweatshirt and pull out a wadded-up red dress.

"It's not what you think," she repeated. Tears welled up, then rolled down her cheeks, and she didn't bother to wipe them away.

Lauren paused, shivering in the gusty wind. What was Leesa up to now? "Where's Jill? What have you done with her?"

Leesa's head jerked up. "I haven't done anything to Jill. I don't know why she missed rehearsal."

"Tell me the truth, or I'm taking the evidence inside right now. You'll be thrown out of the play." She shook the wig hard, and bits of popcorn flew out of it. "And if you've hurt Jill, I'll get you arrested."

"Okay, okay." Leesa shook out the wrinkled

dress. "Jill's fine. She's coming late, that's all." She paused. "She thought rehearsal was at 10:30."

"No, she didn't. I talked to her Wednesday and she had the right time."

Leesa scraped her boot back and forth on the gravel drive. "I left a message on her answering machine that the rehearsal time was changed."

"So she'd come when it's all over." Lauren spoke through gritted teeth. "I don't get you. You're smart, you're pretty, you have the neatest clothes, the most friends of anybody in our grade. You've performed and danced lots in the past. Why couldn't you leave Jill alone? She's never had anything neat like this happen to her."

Leesa turned her back abruptly, standing stiffly. Her narrow shoulders shook.

Lauren sighed. "Can you give me one good reason why I shouldn't go inside and tell the whole group what you've done?" she asked.

"No." Leesa's voice was barely audible. She turned around, but her eyes shifted away from Lauren. "But if you knew how important being Annie was to me, you'd understand."

Lauren doubted that, but said, "Okay, you've got one minute to tell me."

Leesa stared at the back of the brick theatre for ten seconds, then spoke. "My dad's leaving us. Right after Christmas. It's been bad at home for a long time."

Lauren blinked, her mouth hanging open. That was the last thing she expected Leesa to say. Was this a put-on? A performance to get her sympathy? Then something clicked in the back of Lauren's mind . . . The shouting in the background when she'd phoned Leesa, the voices Leesa had claimed were from the TV. And Monday morning in the principal's office when a "family emergency" had made Leesa tardy again. She'd been crying that day too. Apparently Perfect Leesa didn't have such a perfect life after all.

"I'm really sorry," Lauren said slowly. "But, well . . . What does that have to do with Jill?"

"She got the part I needed." Leesa chewed her bottom lip. "If I'd landed the lead, Dad would have been so proud of me that he couldn't leave." She smiled crookedly for a second, a very shaky smile. "He calls me his own Shirley Temple. He loves seeing me perform. I know he'd stay if I were the star."

"So that's why you invented that tap dance with the stuffed dog?"

Leesa nodded. "If I couldn't be Annie, then at least I could start the show off with a solo song and dance. That might have worked. Being in the Orphan Chorus isn't good enough though. I asked him, but he won't come to the musical at all now."

Lauren didn't know what to say. Imagine having a dad like that!

Leesa held up the dress. "I'll iron it and bring it back," she said. "Please don't tell. I know you won't believe me, but I was really glad Jill didn't get hurt by the Christmas tree. I couldn't believe I did that. I never wanted her to get hurt. I only wanted a chance to do one performance. I've studied her lines for weeks. I could have stepped in if there was an emergency."

"That isn't all you did." Lauren crossed her arms tightly against the cold. "I think trying to make Jill look like a thief was just as bad."

"What are you talking about?"

"Remember your missing necklace?"

Leesa seemed honestly puzzled. "What about it? You said you found it hidden in a tobacco can."

Lauren pointed a shaking finger at Leesa. "*You* said Jill *stole* it and I was covering for her."

"Okay, I shouldn't have said that about Jill, but I love that locket! I almost died when I thought it was lost."

"What about scaring the little kids in the play, turning out the lights, and messing with props, and pinning nasty notes to the wall, and making them think there was a ghost?"

"But— But—" Leesa's eyes flashed. She threw the wrinkled dress at Lauren, and it landed on the ground. "I didn't do that stuff! I didn't try to scare any little kids into quitting. Why would I? I wasn't out to wreck the whole play. I only wanted Jill to quit so I could be the star."

Lauren picked up the dress and wrapped the wig in it, silent as she considered Leesa's words. That did make sense. Oddly enough, she believed Leesa. There wasn't any reason for Leesa to ruin the whole play. But if Leesa wasn't the mean-spirited phantom, who was?

More importantly, was this "spook" still around, waiting to play one more disastrous trick—on Opening Night?

CHAPTER TWELVE

"Opening Night"

That night at 6:00 while several hundred towns-people gathered around the huge Christmas tree in the middle of the intersection for the Tree Lighting ceremony and Christmas carols, Lauren was battling butterflies in her stomach. She watched the ceremony from the chilly theatre lobby as someone threw a switch and lit the tree while a group dressed as old-time carolers burst into "Hark, the Herald Angels Sing."

A cold wind blew in the gap between the glass doors, and Lauren rubbed her bare arms. She was dressed more for April than late November. Her orphan costume consisted of a thin loose cotton dress covered by a pinafore apron. Her legs were bare above her black socks and lace-up boots. In her arm was a stack of thirty *Annie, jr.* programs, ready to hand out after people bought their tickets. With her face smudged with charcoal and this patched dress, Lauren hoped people could tell she was part of the cast and not some bum that wandered in out of the cold.

"Hey, kid, how you doing?" Nick said behind her, coming through the red and white doors from the inner lobby. Dressed in sharply creased black slacks, a pleated white shirt, and a red bow tie, he looked exactly like the picture of the ushers in the play book. Now Lauren *really* felt like a bum. Why couldn't she have had a pretty costume to wear?

"I'm cold, but mostly it's nerves." *And having you standing beside me looking like a movie star.* Lauren glanced outside at the Christmas tree, then back at Nick. "I wonder how Jill's feeling. Have you seen her?"

"Earlier. I suppose she's in the dressing room." He leaned against the tall, skinny ticket booth as the carolers outside sang "Angels we have heard on high . . ." "A minute ago I was in the makeup room—over in the basement of City Hall—and you should see all the scared little kids. One girl vomited twice on her mom. She might have to go home."

Thinking of throwing up, Lauren's own butterflies batted against her ribs and flew up into her throat. She swallowed hard. "I'm glad I'm not four years old and facing an audience. Stage fright is hard enough at my age." *Oh, why did I say that?* Lauren moaned inwardly. *I sounded like such a baby!*

Nick moved to stand by her at the glass doors. "When will this tree lighting thing wrap up?" he asked. "We never had anything like this in Detroit."

"Pretty soon. Santa brings some candy first, then I think they're done."

Just then Miss Roberts pulled back the short red curtains inside the ticket booth. "Hello, you two," she said, uncovering the opening in the glass where she'd take money later. "Got your programs?" Her voice sounded hollow as it came through the half-circle cut in the glass.

Nick and Lauren both held up their programs. "The tree lighting's almost over," Nick said. "Do you need me to do anything else?"

"Not that I know of," she said, peering between the two signs in the booth window that said **Theatre Post Cards for sale 25 cents** and **All Seats 2.50.** "You've done so much already. You were such a help with the programs, and putting up signs around town, and working on the sets, and collecting money for the *Annie, jr.* sweatshirts." She opened her cash box and broke open rolls of quarters, letting them clatter into the tin box.

"It was fun," Nick said. "I've never been a part of something like this. I just wish . . ." Abruptly he turned away.

Lauren stared down at her programs. She bet he almost said that he wished his mom could be there too.

Just then, Mrs. D. opened one of the inner doors. "Oh, good, you're here," she said to Nick. "Is your car around?"

"Parked out back."

"Could you do me a really big favor? Megan forgot the red leash we're borrowing for Sandy. Megan's already in costume. She left the leash on her front porch and no one's home. Could you go get it?"

"No problem. Where does she live?" Nick handed his programs to Lauren, winked, and left with Mrs. D.

Miss Roberts closed her cash box and tapped on the glass. "I'll grab one of the other orphans to help you till Nick gets back."

"Okay. Thanks."

Alone, Lauren marched back and forth in the tiny outer lobby, trying to keep warm. Frigid air seeped through the cracks between the glass doors, and gave her goose bumps all over. As she paced, her foot kicked a red cylinder-shaped can of fine sand, there for putting out cigarettes. Turning, she glanced overhead at the two giant silver-painted masks, one smiling, the other crying, that hung over the doors.

Back and forth, from the poster of "Coming Attractions" on one side to the concession window on the other, Lauren paced. Thumb-tacked on the "Currently in Release" bulletin board was their *Annie, jr.* poster. Less than an hour before show time!

From outside, a chorus of "Oh Christmas Tree, Oh Christmas Tree" floated on the air. Lauren peered out the door. Gentle flakes of snow were falling, melting as they hit the sidewalk. Perfect! A dusting of snow over the colored lights always made the tree extra beautiful.

Trying to take her mind off the performance, Lauren studied the red indoor-outdoor carpeting below her feet, then the molded light blue ceiling overhead. Each square in the ceiling held a round light bulb. In the center was a white ceiling fan, motionless this time of year.

Glancing over her shoulder to be sure no one was watching, she stepped up to the empty concession window and announced, "I'll have a large box of popcorn, a Green River, and Junior Mints." Even though it cost 25 cents more for Cherry or Green River, that's what she always ordered. Sitting on top of the pop machine were the red and green jugs of flavoring, waiting for the next movie. Too bad that the concession window wouldn't be open for *Annie, jr.*

Lauren pressed her nose to the small window and stared inside. The vacant room held an old desk, brown wooden shelves of Skittles, Rolos and suckers. Next to the ice machine just inside the window, the scrubbed popcorn popper sat silent. Red and white striped popcorn boxes, two different sizes, were stacked alongside. Lauren usually bought the 75-cent size, but when she and Jill came together, they split the big one for $1.75.

Just then a blast of cold air made her jump. People were coming in already!

However, when she turned, it was Barry, brushing snow off his shoulders. Lauren glanced outside. It was starting to collect on the sidewalk now.

"Hi, there," Barry said. "Ready for business?"

"Almost. Miss Roberts is selling tickets. She'll be right back." Lauren grinned. "I'm surprised you came."

"Don't seem like the musical type?" he asked.

"Well . . ."

"Actually you're right. I just thought I'd make my presence known tonight." He glanced in the empty ticket booth, then the empty concession room. "I've heard rumors of odd things happening here lately—accidents and the like. Seemed like a good idea to be on hand tonight."

"I'm glad you are." Lauren nodded. "By the way, have you found who tricked Tillie and Henry out of their money?"

"I've got a couple good leads. Con artists are

slippery fellows, though. They have to be good actors to pull off their swindles."

"Actors?"

"Sure. They're playing a part, convincing people they're someone they're not. You know, like the guy who dressed as a soldier." He glanced at the posters of coming attractions. "All swindlers tend to be outgoing and appear eager to help people."

"Like the guy collecting money for the Food Pantry?"

"Exactly. Con men are smart. They use their brains instead of force to steal."

"But why would they do such things to old people?" Lauren asked, remembering the anguish on Tillie's face at the loss of Leo's ring.

"Money's the reason, pure and simple. Con artists are motivated by that one thing. The elderly are easy targets because of their age and how they trust others." He glanced outside. "Snow's heavier. Supposed to get a couple inches by midnight. Looks like the tree lighting ceremony is over."

Lauren looked down the street. Sure enough, people were drifting in the direction of the theatre. Her stomach leaped into her throat, then plunged down to her toes. In spite of the chilly lobby, she broke out in a sweat.

Just then Miss Roberts returned to the ticket booth, and Jason joined Lauren to help hand out programs. Dressed in ragged shorts and shirt, plus the same socks and lace-up boots, he looked like half the Orphan Chorus. His face and legs were smudged like Lauren's, and she felt more comfortable handing out programs now.

Barry stepped up to buy his ticket, then turned to Lauren for a program. "At least you get a front row seat," she said, laughing.

"I'll probably stand at the back where I can observe the room," he said. "Good luck!"

"Thanks." Just then the double doors swung open, bringing in a swirl of falling snow along with a dozen parents and grandparents. For the next half hour a steady stream of people poured into the theatre. Lauren had no time to think about being nervous as dozens of people surged inside, purchased tickets, and were directed into the theatre.

At one point, Nick returned to see if she needed help, then left again to assist Carl with the props. Lauren only had a dozen programs left, and the crowd had thinned to a trickle. Lauren realized it must be near show time.

"How long should we stay out here?" she asked Miss Roberts.

"Five more minutes should do it." Just then, Mr. Blue stepped inside the tiny ticket booth behind Miss Roberts and tapped her on the shoulder. "Phone call backstage for you," he said. "Sounds important." Then he disappeared.

"Oh dear," she said, shutting the cash box and stashing it on a shelf below the counter. "I'll be right back, Lauren. Tell anyone else who comes that I'll be back in two minutes." She placed the block of wood in front of the opening in the glass, then pulled the red curtains closed.

Only three last minute people showed up while Miss Roberts was gone, and they chatted with Lauren and Jason till she returned. When Miss Roberts whipped open the curtains, she tapped on the glass. "Lauren. Jason. Leave me your programs, and I'll hand them out. Mrs. D. wants you backstage now." She grinned at them. "Looks like a sold-out performance. Now break a leg!"

Lauren wiped her sweaty palms on her dress and handed over her few remaining programs. She knew "break a leg" was theatre talk for "good luck," but it sure didn't make any sense to her. She prayed that *nobody* broke a leg that night—or anything else.

Opening the red and white door, she stepped into the inner carpeted lobby that ran behind the ticket booth. Hurrying down the side aisle behind Jason, Lauren tried to ignore the overflowing crowd of excited parents, grandparents, sisters and brothers. She knew that her own family—minus Shawn, she hoped—was there somewhere, but her quick nervous glances couldn't pick them out.

Lauren realized she'd better go to the bathroom before she sang. So instead of going directly backstage, she ran down the short flight of steps to the rest room. The door was closed, and two other girls waited in line.

"You'd better go to the other bathroom," the first little girl said. "Mrs. D. said we'll start in a minute."

Lauren bit her top lip. The last thing she wanted to do was parade back through the full theatre to the main ladies room. "Tell Mrs. D. where I went, if she asks," she said, deciding quickly.

Back in the main theatre, Lauren strode up the side aisle with her head down, avoiding people's stares. At the back, she noticed Barry talking with Todd, the theatre owner. She bypassed them and hurried to the stairs leading down to the bathroom. *Good!* she thought. It was empty.

A minute later while washing her hands, Lauren heard the door open at the top of the stairs. Sounds of the chattering audience were heard, then hushed when the door closed. Two women were talking as they came down the stairs. Lauren noticed the worried tone of their voices before she actually heard the co-producers' words.

" . . . thrilled, of course, about selling out," Miss Roberts said. "But what should I do about the money?"

"You're sure there were three fifty-dollar bills in the cash box?" Janey Miller asked.

"Absolutely! I remember the three men who each paid for about ten family members." Their anxious voices grew louder as they neared the bottom of the stairs.

"When could it have disappeared, though?" Janey asked. "Weren't you with the money the whole time?"

They paused on the steps. "Oh, my word. Of course." Miss Roberts gasped. "Mr. Blue said I had a phone call backstage just before the play started. I closed the curtain in the ticket booth and ran backstage, but when I said hello, there was a *click* as the line went dead. In all the rush, I'd forgotten."

"*Mr. Blue?* You think the stage manager faked a phone call to get you away from the ticket booth?"

"I never thought of that till just now. Surely it wasn't—" Just then they reached the bottom of the stairs.

Lauren yanked down a paper towel. When the co-producers came around the corner, Lauren tossed her crumpled paper towel in the trash and pretended not to have heard them. "The other bathroom had a line," she explained. "I hope I'm not late!"

"You're fine." Miss Roberts wore a quizzical expression. Worry had cut deep lines across her forehead. "You'd better hurry."

Lauren took the carpeted steps two at a time. As she raced down the aisle once again, Miss Roberts' words—and Barry's—bounced in her brain. Disjointed words tumbled around in her mind, colliding with each other, but she didn't have time to pin them down. Lauren had never considered Mr. Blue! He'd certainly had the opportunity to steal the ticket money, and mess with the props and lights, and loosen the rope holding the upside down tree. But why? Did he really resent them that much? When she arrived backstage, the Orphan Chorus was lined up, ready for the plush red curtain to rise.

Squeezing into her place at the back, she breathed deeply to calm her racing heart and concentrated on the words to "Maybe." Thirty seconds later, the curtain slowly rose, and she was temporarily blinded by the floodlights overhead and the footlights below. The only person in the audience she recognized was Elayna, sitting at the end of the front row taking notes.

Although she didn't miss a word to the opening song, Lauren could barely remember singing it when they finished five minutes later. So many dark thoughts swirled through her mind that she was barely aware of the changing scenes.

One hundred fifty dollars was missing from the

ticket sales! First she'd had money stolen at school, then the old people at Bethany Manor had been hit even harder. Now the theatre. According to Barry, the theatre at least made sense. He'd said the con artists had to be "good actors." Lauren frowned, her jaw tense. Barry might be there to watch for "spooky" happenings, but one thing was certain. Whoever was stealing the town blind was no ghost.

No phantom she'd ever heard of needed cold, hard cash.

At the end of "Hard-Knock Life" Lauren shuffled with the rest of the Orphan Chorus out the side door into the falling snow, then ran to the back door of the City Hall. Inside, they all trooped downstairs to the basement, set up as a dressing room and makeup room. Lauren spotted Carl in a corner and headed over there. Josh's mom was gluing on his mustache for his scene as the laundry man, Mr. Bundles.

"Hold *still*, Carl," Josh's mom said as Lauren approached. "Your mustache will slip if it isn't glued down tight." She pressed hard on one end. "How did you manage to get this thing so bent up anyway?"

"I stuck it in my pocket."

Lauren turned at the sound of more footsteps on the stairs. Elayna peeked into the dressing room, spotted Lauren, and came over. "The musical's a smash! You're all doing such a wonderful job." She glanced around, then scribbled something in her notebook. "Your director said I could come down here, if I wanted."

"I saw you sitting in the front row by the EXIT."

"Made it easy to slip out between acts. Isn't the

snow pretty outside? It's too bad I can't bring my mom out for something like this."

"I know. Tillie'd love it too."

"Wouldn't she though? That's so sad about her, first her ring, then giving her money to that soldier." She shook her head. "Of course, at her age, I'd fall for any line delivered by a cute soldier with blond curly hair and a mustache."

Lauren frowned and waved absent-mindedly as Elayna went off to talk to Carl. Something buzzed like a pesky fly around the back of her mind, something about the phony soldier's description, something . . .

Then she knew. Tillie and Alma had said he had curly hair, a mustache, an Army uniform, and boots with big heels.

While the chorus lined up to march back to the theatre, Lauren's mind was in a whirl. Of course! Barry said con artists had to be great *actors*. She glanced around the makeup room. And what did actors wear? Disguises. Mustaches. Curly wigs. Glasses, too, she thought, recalling the boy with the limp and glasses who'd collected money for the Food Pantry. *And costumes!*

She recalled the King Kong dressing room when hunting for the laundry man's uniform. On the rack of costumes had been white coats, rubber dolphin outfits, a marching band uniform, a fireman's coat, and *an Army uniform!* Finding heavy boots with big heels would have been a snap—all the orphans wore them, and they came in all sizes. And there were even mustaches in the lavender makeup case!

As the sickening truth sank in, Lauren wanted to run and hide. With sudden clarity, she remem-

bered the Friday before. She hadn't left her backpack unattended at school for more than five minutes. But she *had* left it in a front row seat that day
at the theatre during rehearsal. Anyone in the play
could have heard her tell Carl about the money she
intended to take to the bank.

Lauren's eyes grew round. She bet she knew
exactly when her money had disappeared: *when the
lights went out during Leesa's dance.* Lauren had
heard steps running overhead in the balcony after
the lights went out. Now she was sure of it. Of
course. Whoever was up there in the lights booth
had run across the balcony, then come down the
stairs on the opposite side of the theatre. By the
time Mrs. D. got upstairs and turned the lights back
on, that person could have easily made it to the
front of the theatre—and taken her money from her
backpack.

There was no escaping the ugly truth. The person who'd swindled Tillie and her friends, and the
thief who'd stolen the ticket money and Leesa's
necklace, plus swiped Lauren's own Christmas
money . . . was *someone she knew.* Maybe someone
in the *Annie, jr.* cast, or the stage manager, Mr.
Blue.

Maybe even a friend.

Shuddering, Lauren walked unseeing through
the heavily falling snow to the back door of the theatre. Inside, she started up the steps to the stage
when an idea flashed through her mind. She pictured the day she'd found Leesa's necklace wrapped
in foil inside the tobacco can on the work bench.
Unless she missed her guess, the ticket money from
the cash box was stashed there right now.

The cash would probably be there till after the play, when the thief would retrieve it. If she waited to grab it, it might be too late.

As the rest of the chorus filed up on stage, Lauren slipped out of line and hung back, than ran downstairs and headed straight to the work bench. The tin Band-Aid box was still there, and still empty. But the tobacco can was gone.

Motionless, Lauren considered hunting for Barry. She started back up the stairs when a scratching noise made her stop. Was she hearing things?

She tiptoed around the swamp cooler and down the dark narrow hallway under the stage, but heard nothing else.

However, when she reached the furnace, she heard another scraping noise, from the poster room this time. A wooden box was being moved, sliding across the rough cement floor. Someone was in there!

Rounding the corner, she spotted him kneeling in front of the box, the tobacco can in his hand. At first she didn't recognize him. He'd changed into shorts and work boots, his outfit for working backstage.

"Stop!" she cried, horrified when he turned around. She just couldn't believe it.

His dark eyes were hard as granite, and Lauren barely recognized him with the ugly snarl on his face. He opened the tobacco can and scooped out the bills. "I'm taking this money, and you can't stop me."

Before Lauren could answer, she was knocked sideways as he pushed past her.

CHAPTER THIRTEEN

"Final Curtain"

As Nick rushed past her, Lauren grabbed at the money, but caught his sleeve instead. He shook her off, but the money went flying. At the same time, something small and shiny skittered across the cement behind the furnace.

"Nick! Stop!" Lauren yelled.

"Leave me alone!" he snarled, bending to scoop up the fifty-dollar bills. When he scrambled behind the furnace for the ring he dropped, Lauren searched for something to stop him. Nick was a foot taller than she was, and also outweighed her by fifty pounds. His wrestler's build would knock her flat if she got in his way.

Then she noticed the row of brooms and shovels hanging on the wall opposite the furnace. Lunging across the room, she grabbed the longest push broom. Holding it in front of her, she blocked his escape toward the swamp cooler. She didn't want to hurt him, just to stop him. Nick started toward her, then backtracked, stuffing money in his pockets.

Oh, no, Lauren thought. *He knows about the hidden door in the poster room!* He'd escape that way. She leaped ahead, reached low with the broom, and caught his ankle. He sprawled face down on the cement floor.

He lay stunned for only a moment. Then, scrambling to his feet, he turned to charge her. There was a terrible welt of dark red across his nose. Lauren felt sick when she saw it.

"Get out of my way!" he said. "*Now.*"

"No." Lauren's voice trembled. She hated doing this, but she had to try. Could she possibly block his escape until "Easy Street" ended? Until the music and dancing stopped no one would hear her scream. If she couldn't stop him, he'd be up the steps and out the EXIT door to the alley in thirty seconds flat.

"I'm leaving. Now!" His voice sounded like the growl and snap of a mean hungry dog. Eyes narrowed, Nick advanced slowly, his free hand ready to grab the broom if she swung again. A goose egg protruded from the middle of his forehead. "Move aside. I don't want to hurt you. You can't stop me."

"Maybe *she* can't," said a deep voice directly behind Lauren, "but I can."

Nick jumped back as Barry stepped from behind the swamp cooler. Barry took the broom from Lauren, then stepped around her and between them. "Give me the money, Son. You don't want to do this."

Nick backed up quickly, panic-stricken. As the blood drained from his face, he clutched the wall for support. He glanced at the crumbling tunnel that wound around under the theatre, then ran the opposite direction toward the poster room.

"It's no use," Barry called. "I've barricaded the other door. You can't get out that way either."

Nick's frantic gaze went from Lauren to Barry to

the money in his hand, then back to Lauren. Lauren's heart constricted when she saw both the pain and the fear in Nick's eyes. Finally, shoulders slumped, he held out the money to Barry.

"What else have you got there?" the young policeman asked, pointing at Nick's pockets.

Silently, Nick dug deep and handed over a soft cloth pouch and the diamond ring still clutched in his hand. Keeping an eye on Nick, Barry loosened the draw string and poured out a gold watch and two necklaces. Overhead, the final chorus of "Easy Street" was met with thunderous applause, while down in the basement, they'd just trapped the phantom thief.

Lauren's knees threatened to buckle. She wasn't as thrilled as she thought she'd be at capturing the culprit.

"You all right?" Barry asked her.

Lauren nodded, swallowing the bile that kept rising in her throat. "How did you happen to come down here?"

"I noticed you weren't in the chorus when the orphans came back on stage." He dropped the jewelry back in the pouch and slipped it in his shirt pocket. "I was coming backstage to look for you. I was on the stairs when I heard you scream."

"Thank goodness." Knees weak, Lauren leaned against the brick wall, then stared at Nick. The tension was thick in the silence. "I want my money back," she finally said, her heart feeling crushed within her, "and then I want something else."

Nick stared blankly as if he barely heard her— or cared.

Having trouble breathing, Lauren cocked her

head to one side. "I want to know why you did it. How could you be mean enough to steal from *old people*? And you heard me tell Carl about my Christmas present money and stole it before I could get to the bank. Why?"

What Lauren also wanted to know, but couldn't bring herself to ask, was, *Did you only pretend to like me? Were you just using me to get information about the nursing home? Did you care about me at all, or just my money?*

Nick didn't move or respond. In the silence, the deep bass voice of Daddy Warbucks blended with Annie's higher voice. Lauren knew this was the scene where Daddy Warbucks discussed adopting Annie for his own. Annie would insist she wanted to find and live with her real parents instead.

Finally Nick blinked, then pointed up at the ceiling. "I'm like Annie."

Lauren frowned. "I don't get it."

"I want to live in my *own* home, with my *own* mom. She needs me." Nick's voice cracked, and he paused and swallowed hard. "She's really bad off, but I know she'd get well if I were home to take care of her. She'll be released from the hospital next week, but she'll be all alone."

"Why's she in the hospital, Son?" Barry asked quietly.

"Cancer treatments. Surgery, then chemo. She's been real sick."

Suddenly, without warning, Nick turned and slammed his fist into the brick wall. Lauren gasped and stared at the blood running down his hand from his gashed knuckles.

"It's all right," Barry said, moving to lay a hand

on Nick's shaking shoulder.

"No one understands," Nick said, his voice cracking. "I have to get home to Detroit. I have to be there when she gets out of the hospital."

"That's why you stole the money?" Lauren asked.

Nick nodded miserably. "I had to do something. I could pawn the jewelry. With the ticket money from this weekend, I would have had enough to make it home. My aunt and uncle won't let me go. They said I need to stay in school. That's what my mom wants too." His voice was tired, and there were heavy bags under his eyes. His eyelids drooped so far over his brown eyes that they almost hid the sadness there.

Lauren untied her pinafore and wrapped it around Nick's bleeding hand. She could understand why he felt driven to get home. She'd want the same thing if it were her own mother. Lauren watched as Barry took Nick's arm and led him down the hall toward the swamp cooler. Nick's backbone stiffened, and he pulled back his shoulders. Was Nick under arrest? Lauren figured he was—or would be soon.

Still in shock, Lauren hung the broom back up on the wall. At least Tillie would get her ring back, and the residents' money would be returned. But with the way things had turned out, it was hard to be happy about it.

She followed Barry and Nick up the steps, then out the side EXIT door. Snow was falling in large clumps now, and the ground was covered. They left fresh tracks as they covered the short distance to City Hall, only Lauren didn't suppose they'd go downstairs to the makeup room. Just beyond City Hall was the police station.

As she watched Barry lead Nick away, Lauren was struck by the fact that things were not at all what they'd seemed: not Leesa and her perfect family, not Nick, not the "nice" soldier at the nursing home . . . She'd made a lot of assumptions, based on what little information she had. Not one of her beliefs had turned out to be true.

Saturday's performance was in the afternoon, and the cast party followed immediately in the Viking Hall above City Hall. The stage moms had decorated the huge room in big rainbow streamers, black musical notes and the song title "Tomorrow!" Lauren surveyed the room with mixed pleasure. Both performances had received standing ovations, but with Nick's arrest, gloom colored the celebration for her.

Lauren's parents were back in the Hall's kitchen right then, unpacking the food ordered by Mrs. D.: sugar cookies frosted with rainbows, dog-shaped cookies frosted in chocolate swirls, double fudge brownies, and cups of rainbow sherbet. They wouldn't let her or Carl help serve either.

"This is your special day," her mom had said when Lauren peeked into the kitchen. "Go out there and enjoy it."

Kids milled around, waiting for food to appear. Before refreshments were the award presentations. "Down in front," Mrs. D. called, waving the parents into folding metal chairs and the kids to the floor. "We have awards for everybody! Please be seated."

With great flourish, she proceeded to call each

performer up front, one by one, for an individually designed certificate. The smaller children received awards like "Best Behaved" and "Nicest Manners" and "Biggest Smile." Lauren's best laugh came when Carl was awarded the "Future Hollywood Heart-Throb." Mrs. D. said that in his Mr. Bundles mustache, he was the "closest thing to Clark Gable she'd ever seen." *Whoever that was,* Lauren thought.

Out of the corner of her eye, Lauren noticed movement on the stairs. Elayna's head appeared as she climbed up the steps from the street. Lauren waved, glad her friend could stop in. She knew Elayna was flying home to New York early the next morning.

"Hi," Lauren whispered when Elayna removed her winter coat and sat cross-legged beside her. "How's Tillie? Did she get her ring back yet?"

Elayna shook her head. "Not yet, but she will. Henry gets his watch back too, and all the money they donated. Nick had saved every penny. Right now, I think it's evidence in the case."

Lauren raised her voice over the applause for Pippin, Mrs. D.'s dog who was given a red neck ribbon for his performance as Sandy. The dog danced and skittered when they clapped, his toe nails clicking on the hard wood floor.

"I still can't believe Nick dressed up in those disguises, even though I understand why, and stole from them," Lauren said, the knots in her stomach tightening. "I wonder what will happen to him."

"I heard that he might get off with a severe warning," Elayna said. "The people at Bethany Manor refused to press charges once they learned he only wanted to go home to take care of his mother. And since the musical gets its ticket money back, they want to drop it too."

Lauren frowned. "How exactly *did* Nick steal the ticket money?"

"I understand that he left the theatre to run an errand before the performance, then ran half a block to the Kum & Go store. He called Miss Roberts from there, then ran back to the theatre and snatched the money while she was backstage."

"So *that's* how he faked the phone call." Lauren pleated the edge of her T-shirt. "Miss Roberts pulled the curtains in the ticket booth when she left, so we never saw Nick go in there."

"Mrs. D. *wasn't* happy to find out he'd messed with the lights to scare people and locked you in the basement to frighten you away from his hiding place. Apparently he hoped the idea of a phantom would distract people from what he was really doing."

"It almost worked. At least I got my Christmas money back," Lauren said. "I'm picking up that Blue Willow platter right after the cast party."

"Great!" Elayna wrapped an arm around Lauren's shoulders and squeezed. Lauren hugged back, glad that Elayna had had nothing to do with the weird happenings at the theatre. She'd simply gone to high school with Todd before moving to New York, so he'd trusted her with a key to come in and look around.

When the awards were all given out, the cast rushed toward the long decorated table near the west windows. Several moms stood guard over the food, counting out cookies, pouring strawberry punch, and sticking plastic spoons in the dishes of sherbet.

Carl found them in line and budged in behind Elayna. "Room for the future Hollywood hearth-throb here?" He bowed and kissed Elayna's hand, and Lauren groaned. Would he never quit?

Elayna pretended to be dizzy with pleasure. "Heart-throbs can budge in line with me anytime."

"Did you hear the latest about Nick?" he asked.

Lauren nodded. "About dropping the charges? I was glad to hear that."

"No, something better." He inched forward a few steps in line, then stopped again. "I guess his aunt and uncle were really mad when they found out, after giving Nick a home and all, but they understood why he did it. They decided to move his mom to Story City next week when she gets out of the hospital. She's going to be living with them until she's stronger."

"Really?" Lauren's heart lightened immediately. Nick would still be living just down the block. Lauren grabbed Carl's arm. "That's such a great solution!"

"I agree," Elayna said. "Say, did you give Lauren her present yet?"

"No, but I have it with me." Carl ran to the coat rack, then came back and handed Lauren a plastic bag. "For you. Merry Christmas early."

Lauren squeezed the soft bag. "Why now?"

"Open it and see. I wanted you to have it before Elayna left for New York."

Lauren pulled a soft tissue-wrapped package from the sack, then handed the sack back to Carl. Ripping off the tape, she unwrapped a bright yellow

Annie, jr. sweatshirt. "Thanks, Carl!" she said. "I really wanted one."

"I knew you couldn't afford one after your money was stolen." He rolled up and down on the balls of his feet. "Turn it over. That's the best part."

Lauren flipped the sweatshirt over. Painted on the back was a giant magnifying glass, the kind that Sherlock Holmes always carried. Underneath it read: "To my favorite detective, Lauren Burk." And it was autographed by Elayna Marie Hayes.

"This is so cool!" Lauren said.

Carl nodded, looking very pleased with himself. "It's one of a kind. Us heart-throbs are original, you know."

"I'll wear it forever," Lauren said, slipping it over her head. But for more than one reason, she didn't require a sweatshirt to remember the play. The nightmare memories of being trapped in the basement of the theatre might eventually fade, but would never disappear.

Yes, Lauren thought, *Annie, jr.* had given a whole new meaning to the term stage fright.